FLIGHT

A

SPEEDSUIT POWERS

STORY

by Allen Paul Weaver III

FLIGHT
A SPEEDSUIT POWERS STORY

By: Allen Paul Weaver III

Conceptual designs for cover art and illustrations created by:
Allen Paul Weaver III / Radiant City Studios, LLC

Cover image designed by:
Allen Paul Weaver III

Cover Layout designed by:
Allen Paul Weaver III

Interior Design:
Allen Paul Weaver III

Illustration drawn by:
Allen Paul Weaver III

Published by: Radiant City Studios, LLC
Books may be ordered by contacting:
Allen Paul Weaver III at **www.AllenPaulWeaver3.com**

ISBN: 978-0-9961045-6-2 (pbk)
Printed in the United States of America

DEDICATION

In memory of Sheree Williams...
(July 15, 1974-July 21, 2015)

You truly were a woman who knew how to fly and how to inspire others to do the same. I am glad we called each other "friend." May your legacy continue to live on within the hearts and minds of everyone you touched.

READ THIS FIRST!

You hold in your hands, the very first book in the Speedsuit Powers Expanded Universe! In this 'Expanded Universe' you will meet new characters, on their own journeys, who live in the same world as Curtis Powers, Treyshawn Jinkins, Kelly Washington and the other characters from the Speedsuit Powers Trilogy.

FLIGHT takes place about three years after the Trilogy ends. You can choose to read FLIGHT as a stand alone story, but it will be *extremely beneficial to you if you read the Trilogy first.* However, if you don't have access to the Trilogy yet, and would like to jump right into FLIGHT, make sure you **begin with the Prologue.** That will provide you with the context.

I hope you enjoy this story! There is so much more to come.

Sincerely,

Allen Paul Weaver III

Author, Speedsuit Powers Trilogy & Flight

Prologue

PRODIGY MAGAZINE. December 2018.

Finally! The next phase of our favorite story is here. Prodigy Magazine brings you the exclusive interview with the one and only, Curtis Powers—widely known around the planet as Jetstream: the world's fastest man.

Three books were written about his amazing journey and covered in great detail: the loss of his father to cancer while in middle school, using his intellect in 9th grade to outwit a school bully (who ultimately became his friend), his world record run in the now famous Mach-1 Speedsuit, a 2012 Olympics appearance, his college career, his efforts to create solutions to school bullying situations, the development of additional powersuits, his kidnapping ordeal, the high-tech exhibitions, the Compressor-X games, a museum, and now the ownership and rise of his own multi-million dollar company!

Prodigy Magazine caught up with Curtis and got him to slow down long enough to talk. Here's what he had to say:

PM: Anyone familiar with your story can see that you faced tremendous odds at such a young age. How do you think you were able to overcome them?

CP: My family, friends and wider community were critical to my success. As well as my faith in God. There were times when I wanted to give up on life because things were so tough, but I had support to get me through the hard times.

PM: Who inspires you?

CP: Wow. How much space do you have? [laughing]. Of course my parents, my brother Omar, my wife Kelly, best friends Treyshawn and Gavin, and of course Mr. Grabowski. These are on the short list. There are a host of others, like Erica Cosway who now heads The Montgomery Group. If I listed everyone else, they would probably take up the rest of the interview!

PM: The Montgomery Group was run by its founder and CEO, Chasm Montgomery up until his tragic passing a few years ago.

CP: Yes. That's correct. Not a day goes by that I don't think about him.

PM: Mr. Montgomery was one of your mentors while you were in college.

CP: Yes. He taught me a lot about creativity, technology and innovation, and how the world works. He also left part of his fortune to me in his Will. That has enabled me to get my company up and running to its current level, as well as engage in philanthropy.

PM: Now, you mentioned your parents. We know your dad had a great impact on your life.

CP: Probably more than anyone else. What made it so wasn't just the time I spent with him before he died, but the fact that he left me a journal with all of the things he wanted to say but knew he wouldn't be around to say. That journal really helped to pull me through some seriously hard times while in college.

PM: So, what have you been up to with your company? We hear you are hiring.

CP: [Laughing]. Word gets around quickly! Business is going well. We've just finished a major hiring campaign and only have a couple of positions left to fill.

PM: We are told one position in particular is connected to you.

CP: Yes. The Senior Special Projects Manager will work directly with me on a host of new endeavors. And these last few candidates are amazing.

PM: Can you give us any hints about who's applying?

CP: Sorry, I can't. [Chuckles]. But I do have my eye on someone who seems to be perfect for the role. I am really excited about where Powersuit Technologies is headed. But I can't share our plans just yet.

PM: In one of your early interviews with Sports Magazine you were asked to share some advice. Here is what you said: *"It's not fun when people make fun of you, but don't let that be an excuse for not doing your best. Try to surround yourself with people who support you, not people who only want to use you."*

CP: Wow! [Laughing]. That was my very first magazine interview. I was still in high school at the time.

PM: Do you still live by your advice?

CP: Sure do! Everyday.

PM: What advice would you like to give our readers today?

CP: [Quietly thinking for a moment]. First, everyone is not going to be happy with you wanting to do something positive in the world.

PM: Why do you say that?

CP: Because I've experienced it first hand. What someone does to try and destory us often leads to our greatest opporutnity for change and growth. However, that opportunity will lead to opposition because for the most part, people want to keep the status quo. I'm not saying opposition is necessarily bad. It's definitley uncomfortable, though. But you need to expect that it will come to your doorstep at some point in your life. If you expect it, you'll be less likely to quit when it arrives. When you view opposition as a stepping stone to help propel you upward, then you can achieve something in life beyond what you thought was possible.

PM: That is a wonderful explanation! What is your second piece of advice?

CP: My second piece of advice is this: Where you come from doesn't have to define nor determine where you are going.

PM: Can you unpack that a bit?

CP: Sure. Many of us think that a strong beginning is the only way to qualify us for a strong ending in life. Everything has to be "together" before we can be successful. While that does work for some, the vast majority—myself included—don't start out with a silver spoon in our mouth. In fact, I think those who have been given a silver spoon are actually the ones at a disadvantage because everything has been handed to them. That's not the way life works. Yes, some things are given, but the rest is created.

Your ability to create isn't determined by whether you were raised in the suburbs, the 'hood, or rural areas. You're access to resources may be somewhat determined by these factors, however, your greatest resource in life is that living computer sitting right behind your eyes. You know, the one that's nestled between your ears. Your mind is the great equalizer. A person with little-to-no resources, but who has developed their mind can run circles around the person who doesn't take the time to develop their mind, even though they may have all the resources in the world.

What makes a person a prodigy isn't only his or her IQ. It's all about how we use the IQs' we've been given. We can all be prodigies in one way or another. We just have to discover that way, that avenue, that path and pursue it with everything we've got. And while you pursue what truly is significant to you, don't forget to help others do the same in their lives.

PM: That is wonderful advice! Thank you so much for your time.

CP: Thank you for the opportunity!

PM: We look forward to seeing what Powersuit Technologies does next!

CP: You know our tagline: "Run. Leap. Soar!"

Chapter One
WAITING TO FLY

"You've never lived until you've flown."
- Bessie Coleman

Thursday. January 10, 2019. 9:00am. Atlanta. Schuyler Watkins sits in her business attire, fumbling with her portfolio briefcase. Her knees quietly knock together while she waits for a job interview with someone who has inspired her for the last seven years. Sunlight fills the room, met by bright and playful colors on the wall which surrounds the prominently displayed company name: Powersuit Technologies - Run. Leap. Soar! She smiles at the realization of her present location and how improbable it was... by other people's standards. Yet, here she sat, at 19 years old, all because of the pursuit of a dream.

The floor seems alive with creative energy as employees walk, talk and work. Yet, her stomach distracts her with a grumble as her face feels flush. A slight sensation of nausea momentarily swells. *Glad I didn't eat anything heavy,* she thinks. *So nervous, I wouldn't be able to keep anything down.* She takes a deep breath and forces a smile as she notices the receptionist studying her expression.

"Are you alright?"

"Uh, yes. Do you have any water?"

Several minutes pass as she finishes her glass. She breathes a sigh of relief as her nervousness fades a bit. Just then, a woman exits from the double glass doors of a nearby conference room and stops.

"Ms. Watkins?" She smiles. "Mr. Powers will see you now."

The assistant walks Schuyler into the conference room. She immediately notices a high-quality poster displayed prominently on the wall. However, her attention is suddenly captured by the wall-to-wall windows overlooking a gorgeous view of the countryside. Schuyler walks over to them and stops at the sight.

"I think it's nice, too."

She turns to find Curtis Powers standing in the corner with a smile. The assistant leaves as Curtis welcomes his guest.

"It's such an honor to meet you, Mr. Powers," Schuyler gushes as she shakes his hand.

"Please," he smiles as they both sit down, "Call me Curtis. And the honor is mine. I know this is a job interview, but I ordered some lunch. Figured we could just sit and talk."

"Sure," Schuyler utters in a slightly nervous pitch. "You've been a hero of mine for a long time... since you set the first world record. Thank you for meeting me."

"We have an open position for a Senior Special Projects Manager," Curtis smiles, "and with your recent achievement, you may be just the person we need. What you were able to accomplish was pretty amazing. I've watched your viral video at least a hundred times and I still can't figure out how you did it."

"Trade secret," Schuyler laughs as her jitters fade away. "Thank you for the compliment."

"With your invention, you could probably write your own ticket. Maybe even create a new extreme sport."

"Like your Compressor-X Games," Schuyler beams. "Those have really taken off."

"Yes they have. And if you have a way to turn your invention into an experience other people would pay to be a part of... then yours could be just as big, if not bigger!"

"Well, I'm not sure about the extreme sport option just yet, but I *have* received a lot of job offers." She pauses with a broad smile. "But I would like to work for you."

"Why me?" Curtis inquires. "Why here? Surely, there are plenty of other places you could have gone to for an employment opportunity."

"Honestly—"

"No. Lie to me," Curtis replies with a straight face.

Schuyler stares at him for a moment, unsure of what to say.

"I'm kidding!" he chuckles. "Honestly... why do you want to work here?"

Schuyler laughs nervously before continuing. "You are right. I could have chosen another option. But none of those places has Curtis Powers at the helm. You created Powersuit Technologies specifically to inspire people. And that's my desire as well... to inspire people.

"You are one of my heroes and I want to learn from you. It also helps that your company sits on a 3-acre state-of-the-art campus with eleven departments, almost 100 employees, an impeccable work-life balance philosophy, and a focus on philanthropy, education and innovation."

Curtis raises his eyebrows with a nod of his head. "Someone has done her research!"

"Never leave home without it," Schuyler laughs before continuing. "What I did earlier this year was just the first part of a life-long dream. I believe you can help me with the second part. And *that* could change the world."

"I see. And what about college? You have solid grades and you have already been accepted by Harvard, MIT, Georgia Tech and several others."

"I plan to go," Schuyler smiles. "Just not yet. I want a few years of real-world experience under my belt first. Learning from you could probably count towards college credits, too."

Curtis sits back in his chair and gazes at his new potential employee. "Is your delay also due to the response from people on the Internet?"

Schuyler's smile diminishes. "You noticed that, huh?"

"A lot of people haven't been kind."

"Oh, they're *way beyond* not being kind. Some of the responses to my video have been brutal. People think they can sit anonymously behind a computer or phone screen and say all kinds of craziness."

"Some people have been trying to disprove your video. They say it's fake and that you used computer generated effects like that guy from a few years back who claimed to have created wings to fly."

Schuyler sits silently. "Well it is real. I could have gone straight to college after graduation, but I took last year to finally pursue this dream. And what hurts are the boatloads of comments, like one guy who said: 'White men with money have been trying to crack the code of personal human flight for centuries and you're telling me some black girl from Brooklyn figured it out? No way this video is real!'"

"How does that make you feel?" Curtis inquires.

"Angry. Hurt. " Schuyler gives a faint smile. "After crying about it, I eventually put that guy's comment up on my wall. Now, I use it for fuel."

"There are people who want to deny the greatness of black people," Curtis admits. "But, we've been responsible for a myriad of inventions that has positively affected societies and cultures for longer than the white guys who have been trying to crack the code on flight."

"I know that," Schuyler agrees, "But it still hurts to know that in 2018, people will work overtime to try and disprove my accomplishments solely

4

because I am a black woman."

"And yet," Curtis replies, "you have helped to inspire scores of young girls. I saw you on television a couple of months back; when you delivered your keynote speech at the Black Girls S.T.E.A.M. Power event. You killed it!"

"I threw up." Schuyler states flatly while shaking her head.

"You did?" Curtis responds surprised. "What happened?"

Thursday November 22, 2018. Black Girls S.T.E.A.M. Power!

Over five thousand girls and their chaperons scream at the top of their lungs as Alicia Keys and her backup singers dance back and forth on an expansive stage. Her musicians play with a ferocious intensity. The lyrics coming from her mouth are those of her hit song, Back To Life.

Schuyler stands offstage mildly watching the phenomenal performance. Amy, the representative assigned to her, rocks back and forth to the music with clipboard in hand. She suddenly stops as instructions come through her earpiece. A moment later, she turns to Schulyer.

"This is Alicia Key's last song. Angela Bassett will come out from the other side of the stage to introduce you. Then you're on!" Amy's expression turns serious as she sees Schuyler's face. "Are you alright Ms. Watkins? Did you hear what I said? You're about to be next after Angela Bassett!"

Schuyler's eyes are wide open as she stares at the crowd. "I—I've never spoken in front of this many people before," she stammers.

"Stage fright," Amy responds with an air of concern. "It happens to everyone," she utters cooly.

Schuyler seems unfazed by the comment. "I'm not sure if I can do this," she blurts out. "The lights... the crowd... what if I forget what to say?"

"Just relax," Amy soothes as she puts her arm around her and smiles warmly. "You can fly through the air on an invention *you* created. Speaking to a *few* girls who want to hear about what you have done shouldn't be too hard. Right?"

Schuyler slowly takes her eyes off of the bright lights and the loud crowd of girls and focuses on Amy. "You're right," she mumbles with a half smile.

"I know," Amy smiles back broadly as she softly rubs Schuyler's back. "Just breathe and you'll be just fine!"

Schuyler smiles just as broadly with a nod of her head before a sudden belch forces its way through her lips. She covers her mouth and grabs her stomach while frantically looking around. A large bucket rests against the wall. She runs over to it.

"No. No. No. No. No...!" Amy utters with a matched urgency as she quickly follows behind Schuyler. "That's not—"

But it's too late...

"—a garbage can." Amy slowly finishes her sentence as she gags while trying to resist the sudden urge to vomit up her breakfast, lunch and the snack she had thirty minutes ago.

Still bent over, Schuyler pulls a napkin out of her back pocket, with a few coughs, and wipes her mouth as she stands upright again. With a deep breath, she smiles. "Sorry about that. I feel better now. Glad this garbage can was here."

"Didn't you hear me?" Amy balks politely. "That's *not* a garbage can."

"It's not?" Schuyler gasps as she turns and looks down into the bucket where bottled drinks float in ice water and chunky vomit. She turns back to Amy with a firghtened and sorrowful look. Amy—clearly red in her face—bursts into laughter. Schuyler laughs as well as both of their eyes begin to tear. Their laughter so overwhelms them that they don't realize the meaning of the crowd's sudden applause: the music has stopped. Alicia Keys and her group quickly walk right pass them and reach into the bucket.

⋂

Atlanta. The Present. Powersuit Technologies. Job Interview.

Curtis almost chokes on his bagel. "That was crazy!"

"I know!" Schuyler laughs hysterically. "I *was* able to stop them though, before they actually *touched* anything. Yuck!"

Curtis laughs heartedly. "Well, like I said, you nailed the speech. If you hadn't said anything, I'd never know you had vomited just minutes before."

"I'm glad. Good thing I didn't get anything on my clothes!"

"Right! Well, I've anaylzed your flight video. And even though I can't figure out *how* you were flying, I do believe you did."

Schuyler smiles broadly. "Thank you. Did you ever have to face this kind of scrutiny with your achievements?"

"I've had haters over the years. There were people who didn't believe that a black boy was capable of creating the Mach-1 Speedsuit. But once they saw it in action and saw it was verified by outside groups, then much of that stopped. But I've always had some diehard critics who try to 'keep hope alive'. They believe that their skewed view was accurate. However, I've never experienced the kind of pushback you have on social media. I'm sorry you have had to go through that."

"Well, it's like you said in your last Prodigy Magazine interview, 'We have to expect opposition to come to our doorstep at some point in our life. That way we won't give up.'"

"So, more research, huh?" Curtis smiles.

"Oh, I'm a stalker like that," Schuyler laughs. "I mean—not a *real stalker*—but when it comes to researching a person or a topic. I like to read as much as I can get my hands on."

Curtis laughs heartily. "You've piqued my interest. And I'm glad you were honest about how you felt."

"But that's one of the reasons why I want to take the time to get some real-world experience with you. Not only can I be a great asset to your company, but working for you will help build my credibility as an inventor."

"Agreed," Curtis nods his head. "Okay, let's move on from the video for a minute. Tell me about your *why*."

"My *why*?"

"Yes. Take me back to the beginning. How did this start for you? Walk me through the adventure."

"Well," she smiles, "it all started when I was six years old."

I'll never forget when I saw him fall...

It was such a beautiful day in Brooklyn. The sky was blue and the white clouds were puffy. Spring had just begun and there was a cool breeze in the air. We arrived back at our building—fresh from the park, where the smell of urine mixed with most things on the playground. Even so, my brother and I laughed easily as daddy carried us in his arms.

People from the neighborhood stood in groups pointing up at a man.

Some screamed and shouted for him not to jump. Others laughed and cajoled him. Someone said his life had fallen apart and he couldn't take it anymore. Sirens were heard in the distance. I was only six years old when I saw him step off the ledge at the top of my apartment building. My dad tried to shield me and my brother's eyes, but we could see between the cracks in his fingers.

I wasn't sure why I felt afraid. Maybe because those around me were. But as the man plummeted to the ground, amidst screams from the street, I couldn't help but think, *Why can't we fly like the birds?* Then came the loud crash. Everybody was so busy looking down as my daddy handed my brother and me to one of our neighbors so he could try to help the man. Then the police and ambulance finally arrived. They were always late where we lived.

Everybody was looking down, but a breeze swept my gaze to the sky. Right then my eyes caught sight of a bird hovering effortlessly on the wind. I strained to watch that bird as it rose higher into the air before veering off behind a nearby building. Just then a thought entered my mind: maybe humans could fly like the birds... someone just had to figure out how. Somehow, at that exact moment, a desire I have never be able to get rid of was planted in my soul... I wanted to fly. I can't explain it, but it was like an invisible hand reached inside my chest and planted this seed of a dream in my heart.

Atlanta. The Present. Powersuit Technologies. Job Interview.

"You wanted to fly."

"Metaphorically and literally... in *every* sense of the word."

Brownsville. Brooklyn.

"Schuyler! Tyler! Breakfast is ready!"

Sister and brother run into the kitchen and quickly sit at the small table as their father, Jacob Watkins, prepares their plates.

"We have to hurry, so I can get you both to school on time," he says while placing the plates on the table. He utters a quick prayer over the food and they dig in.

"Daddy?"

"Yeah, Baby?"

"I want to fly."

"Like in an airplane?"

"No. Like a bird."

Eggs shoot out of her brother's mouth as he laughs.

"Tyler!" Jacob exclaims, "you're making a mess!"

"Sorry, Daddy," Tyler muffles his mouth and quickly swallows. "People can't fly, Schuyler! We don't have wings!"

"Well, maybe I'll make some!" she scoffs.

"You'll just fall to the ground like the man did last week!"

"Okay, that's enough Tyler," Jacob interjects. "We already spoke about last week. That is nothing to laugh about."

"Well maybe if he had wings," Schuyler replies, "then he wouldn't have fallen and died."

Jacob sighs hard. "Okay, both of you promise me that you will *not* try to make wings and jump from this or any other building."

"We promise," they reply in unison.

"Daddy?" Schuyler asks. "Why did he jump?"

"We talked about this," Jacob replies. "Sometimes life gets really hard and some people can't take it anymore. They think it would be better not to be here. But... that's not true. When things get hard, we just have to keep pressing forward. Eventually, things will get better."

"Is that why mommy isn't here?" Tyler asks. "We were too hard for her?"

Jacob looks at his two children intently with a mix of sudden sadness and compassion. "I know it's hard for you to understand, but sometimes mommies have a hard time after they give birth to a child."

"We made her run away," Schuyler adds.

"No. Her not being here is because she needed to go someplace where she could get help so she could get better. Neither of you did anything wrong. So, we just keep pressing forward. Okay?"

They both nod in quiet agreement as they look down at their plates.

"Is she ever coming back?" Tyler asks.

"I... I don't know. Keep eating or we'll be late. I'm working a double shift, so Auntie will pick you up from school this afternoon. She'll stay here with you until I come home from work tomorrow evening."

"Why do you have to work so many hours?" Tyler inquires.

"I have to do what I can to pay the bills and take care of you two. And it's a good thing we have some family and close friends nearby to help, cause you both have *a lot* of energy!"

The three of them laugh.

"Go brush your teeth and make sure everything you need is in your book bags. It's time to go."

Minutes pass as the trio finishes getting ready and makes their way to the front door. They exit their apartment as Jacob closes the door and engages three locks. Now comes the long wait for the elevator and then the slow descent to the lobby. Once outside the building, they walk expeditiously to the bus stop. A moment later, they push onto the already crowded bus and ride the seven stops to their school.

The laughter of kids can be heard as they exit the bus and walk to the front of the school. A siren chirps as Jacob turns to see his partner sitting in the driver's seat of a double-parked ambulance. Jacob and the kids wave as he rushes them inside to their classroom. He hugs them and sends Tyler into the class first as the late bell rings.

"Schuyler," he smiles as he kneels down to her level. "About you wanting to fly... I'm not saying it is impossible. But the first thing you need to do is study everything that flies—birds, insects, planes, helicopters—everything. That way you can understand how wings work to overcome gravity. So, when you go to the school library today, get some books on those things. And if you can't find any good books there, maybe this weekend we can all take a trip to the big library downtown."

"Thanks Daddy!" Schuyler hugs her father tightly and kisses his cheek before running into her classroom.

Two nights later Jacob quietly enters his apartment and collapses on the couch. His sister, Takeisha, comes out of the bathroom.

"You're finally home."

"Thanks for keeping them the extra time."

"I had to use one of my vacation days to cover it."

"I owe you."

"Oh, yes you do. What happened?"

"The last couple of nights were just crazier than most. Never seen so many gunshot wounds, stabbings and car accidents. First time I had to work a triple shift because one of the guys called out. How are the kids?"

"They are good. Although, apparently, Schuyler was sad because some of the other kids were making fun of her. She said something about wanting to fly like a bird?"

"Yeah. She told me about that."

"Apparently, her friends asked her why she was checking out books on birds and insects. She told them about wanting to fly and... your son... began to tease her. The rest of them followed."

"They shared the womb for 9 months and Tyler was born three minutes before her," Jacob huffs. "Why does that boy have to do the *opposite* of everything she does?"

"Sibling rivalry starts young," Takeisha replies with a deep breath. "Says so in the Bible."

"Yeah, well, it didn't end well for one set. And there was a lot of drama for the other."

"I'm sure things will even out with Tyler."

"I hope so."

"And I hear you are taking them to the library tomorrow?"

"Oh, I forgot about that."

"Your daughter said there weren't enough good books on flight at the school library."

"I'm surprised she found what she did, considering the decreased budget. It's amazing the school still has a library at all."

ဂ

Early Saturday morning finds Jacob and Schuyler sitting at the kitchen table making paper airplanes. Tyler is still sleeping.

"This book on paper airplanes is so cool!" Schuyler exclaims as her father helps her fold her paper with precision.

"I used to make a mean paper airplane when I was younger," Jacob smiles as he reminisces about his youth.

After making a number of different designs, and flying them across the living room, they eventually wake Tyler up and get ready for their trip downtown. An overcast sky greets the Watkins trio as they make their way to the public library. After a couple of hours, Schuyler has an armful of books while Tyler only has two books on motorcycles and a superhero graphic novel.

"I don't understand why you don't like to read, Tyler." Jacob huffs as he looks at the difference in the number of books his children have. "You read very well."

"Reading is boring," Tyler replies. "Unless it's reading about things I like. My friends feel like that too."

"Yeah, well, just because your friends feel that way too, doesn't mean it's right. There's a whole world you can discover in books! Actually, you can discover a whole lot about *a bunch of different worlds* in books!"

14

Jacob has several books in his hand: a couple on medicine and medical emergency practices, a couple of books on science for Tyler and two additional books for Schuyler.

"I found two books you might like about two women who were pioneers in flight."

"What's a pioneer?"

"Someone who does something that no one has done before."

"Great! Who are they?"

"Bessie Coleman was the first African American woman to learn how to fly an airplane and get her pilot's license. And Amelia Earhart was the first woman to fly by herself across the Atlantic Ocean. If you're going to be a pioneer, then it's good to learn about other pioneers."

Schuyler stops walking and looks at her dad as he continues to walk before noticing she is no longer by his side. He turns to see her staring at him. Tyler turns around as well.

"Baby, what's wrong?" Jacob asks as he walks back to his daughter.

"Daddy," Schuyler replies. "Do you really think I can be a pioneer like those women in these books?"

Jacob smiles broadly as he kneels to her level, places his books on the sidewalk and puts his hands firmly on her shoulders.

"Schuyler, you are *already* a pioneer. Nobody I know dreams of flight like you do."

Tyler sucks his teeth as he looks away. Before he realizes, his dad is pulling him close.

"Son," Jacob utters with a warm seriousness as he gazes into Tyler's eyes, "you can be a pioneer, too, if you're willing to blaze your own path by working up to your potential."

Jacob pulls both of his children together in front of him and stares intently into their eyes. "If you *both* apply yourselves, you will be surprised at what you're capable of accomplishing in this life."

𝆑

Thursday November 22, 2018. Black Girls S.T.E.A.M. Power!

Schuyler stands at the podium looking out beyond the glare of the lights into the packed auditorium. The clapping has just ceased as the audience awaits her first words. She scans the first few rows and locks eyes with several young girls.

"My father once told me, 'If you're going to be a pioneer, then it's good to learn about other pioneers...' A pioneer is someone who does something that no one has done before. In a very real sense, all of you here tonight are pioneers because each of you are doing something that no one else has done before... you are living your own life.

"No one can live your unique life but you. We can have similar experiences. We can learn from each other's experience. We can be impacted by one another's experiences. But at the beginning, middle and end of the day, only YOU can live out YOUR experience. What does this mean? It means that your choices and decisions matter because they affect the trajectory which your life can take.

"I stand here before you because I can fly. *Technically*, my invention enables me to glide from a higher elevation to the ground and land without a parachute. Let me also add that my flight harness is a complex system. I am not just tying a blanket around my neck. Having said that, I cannot stand on the ground and rise into the air and truly soar like a bird... yet. But one day in the near future, I am sure I will."

16

The crowd applauds.

"The truth is, we are surrounded by black girls and women who fly every day. From the girl who starts her own lemonade stand to those who become lawyers, doctors, gymnasts, dancers, hairstylists, actors, engineers, firefighters, police officers, teachers, entreprenuers, and a host of other professions.

"And even if we have never met a black woman with a professional career, we see strong black pioneering women in our own homes and neighborhoods. These women are our mothers, grandmothers, aunts, and cousins. These pioneers are also the women in the neighborhood who may not be related to us by blood, but they still look out for us as if we were part of their own family."

The crowd applauds again.

"Now, I can't stand here and tell you that my success has come because of my mother. She and my father divorced when my brother and I were little. So, I know what it is like to not have a strong maternal presence in my life. But, it was my father who raised my brother and me. And it was my aunt, his sister, who helped him when he needed her. So, even if the examples around you are not ideal, you can still learn from each and every situation. I will say that my mother is back in our lives and her presence has really impacted us for the better."

The crowd applauds.

"As I close, let me say this: In my case, flying is both metaphorical and literal. By metaphorical I mean that I desire to be successful in whatever endeavors my hands find to do. But I do realize that in order to fly, I must overcome gravity.

"In order for you to fly, you must overcome gravity, too. You must overcome the gravity that is created every time someone underestimates your ability and declares you can't do something. You must overcome the gravity that is created every time someone says you are not intelligent enough, passionate enough, committed enough, or talented enough. You must overcome gravity every time someone laughs at your pursuit and scorns your attempt to rise above where you are right now.

"The truth is, just like gravity is a natural law which is always present, there will always be the gravity of people's opinions pulling on us. But we must learn how to use it to fuel our desire to fly. What enables a bird, insect, airplane or helicopter to fly through the air? It's not that gravity is turned off for these things. It is that another law is at work— the law of Lift. When the bird, insect, airplane and helicopter meet the requirements necessary to utilize the Law of Lift, then they are able to overome gravity!

"You can overcome gravity and make it work for you! If you discover the requirements for Lift to work in your life, then you will impact this world in ways we can only imagine! Know that you can accomplish almost anything if you are willing to put in the hard work to research, design and create the world you want to see. And if you choose to use me as an example of what's possible, know that it *is* possible for a black girl to learn how to fly! You all have STEAM Power! And if you apply yourselves, you will be surprised at what you will be able to accomplish in this life! I look forward to seeing what YOU do to impact this world for the better! Thank you!"

Schuyler receives a standing ovation from everyone in the auditorium. Amy meets her with a huge hug when she comes off stage.

"That was absolutely amazing! I was really moved by what you said. And don't worry... I won't say a word about our little puking incident."

After the event ends, Schuyler spends an hour signing autographs and listening to young girls and grown women passionately share about their dreams.

Chapter Two

GRAVITY PULLS

"Gravity is ALWAYS pulling us down. Maybe that's why the possibility of flight seems so foreign to some and so spectacular to others."
- Anonymous

Glee smothers the faces of eight kids as glass shatters and dents form on the sides of old car doors. The youth, ranging from 9 to 11 stand, slightly hidden, in an abandoned lot filled with old junk and plenty of rocks of all shapes and sizes. One-by-one five boys hurl their stony projectiles wth amazing accuracy. Two girls follow, with a less than stellar trajectory. Finally, Schuyler launches her arm and releases her grip at full extension. With the beauty of a soaring eagle her paper airplane leaves her hand and glides speedily across the lot and beyond the tattered pile of metal being used as target practice.

"I still don't get you, Schuyler," Charles declares as they all look at her in disbelief. "Why can't you do normal things like the rest of us?"

"Throwing an airplane is normal." Schuyler shrugs.

"Not when we throwing rocks!" Matthias scoffs.

"She's been talking about flight for four years," Tyler adds with a roll of his eyes. "I can't get her to shut up about it."

"Nope!" Schuyler smiles. "Did you know if a golf ball didn't have those dimples in it, it would be less aerodynamic and wouldn't fly as far when it was hit by a golf club?"

"Ugh, another flight-fact," one of the girls declares.

"Why you talkin' about golf balls?" Cory balks. "Nobody here plays golf!"

"I ain't never even seen a golf ball before," Rachelle admits.

"I did one time at putt-putt golf," Vincent shares.

"That don't count," Cory counters with a laugh.

"Well, *I've* seen a real golf ball before," Schuyler answers.

"Our dad got her one for her birthday last week," Tyler adds.

"It's *so* cool," she smiles, "I've been studying them for the last couple of months."

"See?" Cory interjects. "That's what I'm talking about. Golf balls? And what about your pet dragonfly?" He yells. "Who has a dragonfly as a pet?"

"Its wing was damaged," Schuyler replies. "I found it in a field and nursed it back to health!"

"I would have picked it apart," Cory retorts. "Or just stomped on it!"

"Hey!" Schuyler yells. "That's not nice!"

"You know, if it wasn't for your brother," Mercedes admits, "we wouldn't hang out with you like we do. Sometimes, you're kind of weird."

"Well, I don't talk about flying anymore than you talk

about music!"

The group laughs.

"She's right about that," one of them says.

"And what about you, Vincent? You're always drawing as much as I talk about airplanes. And you, Matthias. You always talk about fighting. And Charles. You always talking about gold chains and stuff. We all like what we like and talk about what we talk about. Why do you laugh because I talk about planes and stuff?"

"Cause, you talk about stuff only white people care about!"

"That's not true! Bessie Coleman was the first black woman to learn how to fly a plane and get her international pilot's license. She flew all over the world and did amazing stunts in her plane. People were like 'wow' wherever she went."

"When was that? Like a gazillion years ago!"

"So? My daddy says we can always learn new things from our history. Just because YOU never seen it or done it before doesn't mean it hasn't been done or can't be done."

Atlanta. The Present. Powersuit Technologies. Job Interview.

"Wow," Curtis chuckles, "you really knew how to stand up for yourself."

"I had to learn how to do that," Schuyler responds. "My dad really helped me. He knew that my dream was different from almost everybody else. We lived in the 'hood. And not a great part of the 'hood, at that. It was one of the worst areas. Crime was so bad sometimes we were living in a constant state of anxiety. When we didn't have money, we tried to hold onto hope. At times, all we had were dreams. But there were a lot of people who couldn't focus on dreams because they were just trying to survive. I really didn't fully understand that at 10 years old, but by the time I was 12, it became clear.

☊

Brownsville. Brooklyn.

Seven friends wait outside of an apartment building for Matthias to arrive. A moment later, he exits.

"Quick. Let's hurry up before my dad gets home."

No sooner are the words out of his mouth, that they turn to see his father walking up the block. They run around the back of the building, hoping to circumvent his arrival, but as they come out on the other side, they are stopped in their tracks.

"You thought I didn't see you?" Matthias' father belches. "School is over for the day. You're supposed to be upstairs."

"We—we were just going to the park for a bit," Matthias responds as the group quickly grows nervous.

Matthias Matthews Sr. looks at each of them. His tall, muscular frame imposes a sense of helplessness on the group as he holds his construction hat in one hand and his lunch container in the other.

"It's not safe at the park. You know a kid just got shot there last week."

"That was last week," Matthias responds.

"So, you acting bold because your friends are here?" his father replies. "None of y'all should be at the park. But I'm not your parent. Matthias, get your butt upstairs. Tell your friends you'll see them tomorrow at school."

"Dad, I want to go with them. Just for a little while."

"You do? Well, you know the routine."

The group looks at each other hesitantly as one whispers to another, "What's the routine?"

"So, your friends don't know? Why don't you tell 'em."

"Just forget it," Matthias grumbles. "I'll see you guys tomorrow."

"No, let's *not* forget it," his father interjects as he puts his construction hat and lunch container on the ground. "You want to go to the park? The question is, *can* you go to the park?"

"I said forget it, alright?" Matthias concedes. "You win!"

Matthias Sr. quickly closes the distance between him and his son and slaps him across his head. The rest of the group stumbles back in fear as the assault continues with another slap to the head.

"Go ahead, Matthias," his father balks. "If you want to go to the park, all you got to do is get past me!"

SLAP!

"You're big enough to make your own decisions now, right?"

SLAP! SLAP!

A tear streams down Matthias' face as he jumps back from his father.

"Dad! I don't want to fight you!"

"But you're big and bad, right? You want to go out into the

danger? What happens when the fight comes to you?"

His father throws a punch towards his face, but Matthias blocks it and roars as he throws a punch of his own. His father easily parries the punch away from his body.

"Good! Good! Let's see what you've learned!"

Matthias launches a flurry of punches and kicks. His friends' terror turns into awe as they watch him move like lightning. But their awe diminishes as his father blocks, sidesteps and counters each blow that is thrown his way. With a swift arm lock, shift of his weight and pivot, Matthias' father throws him to the ground—hard. Then he addresses the entire group.

"I know you think I'm harsh. But you ain't got time to play when life is serious. You ain't got time for dreams when people walking around with guns and knives. You got to be able to survive! Craziness happens at all times a day now… but especially at night."

He motions towards his son as he snatches him up from the ground and stands him to his feet.

"What do I keep telling you? *Situational awareness!* These streets will eat you alive if you let 'em. I'm just trying to make you strong—stronger than everybody else. And when you get knocked down, you get your butt right back up!"

He picks up his construction hat and lunch container and turns back towards the group. "Y'all go home."

The next day…

Matthias sits in the school cafeteria with his friends. An intimate conversation takes place amidst the roar of other students.

"I know yesterday was tough to watch… My dad grew up on the streets. Literally. And he's been studying martial arts his whole life. Almost every day of my life my dad would tell me to be aware of my surroundings. When I was eight, he drove me twenty minutes away to the other side of Brooklyn and left me there. He said, 'you find your way home. And don't talk to no cops.' After he drove off, I spent the first ten minutes crying. Then I wiped my eyes and started to try and figure out which direction I needed to go. It took me six hours to get home."

"What happened when you got home?" Cory inquires.

"He asked me if I was okay. I told him yes. He gave me some food to eat and sent me to bed."

"That was four years ago," Cory says. "How come you ain't never told us before?"

"I dunno," Matthias shrugs. "That was a scary time. I don't like thinking about it. But yesterday was just as scary for me."

"You were scared?" Mercedes asks.

Matthias barely nods his head.

"Shoot," Tyler responds, "we were *all* scared. Your dad is no joke!"

Everybody sits quietly as Matthias looks over and sees Vincent drawing.

"Yo! Did you just draw that?" Matthias exclaims as everybody turns to see.

"Yeah," Vincent replies as he holds it up.

The group of friends look in awe at the picture. Vincent has recreated the scene from the previous day, when Matthias and his father were fighting. Every detail is present: from the ripples in their clothes to the clenched tension of the muscles. The entire environment has been drawn too, including them.

"Man," Cory says, "I knew you could draw, but *that* is crazy!"

"Yeah!" Tyler adds. "You've been holding back on us!"

"I think I got a photographic memory," Vincent admits sheepishly. "I just realized a few months ago I could draw whatever I see when I picture it in my mind."

"We should call you Vangogh," Schuyler beams.

"Vangogh?" Matthias interjects. "Who's that?"

"He's one of the most famous artists from the 1800's," Vincent replies.

"How do you know about him?" Mercedes asks.

"My mom's an artist. She learned about him in college when she took a trip to France. She named me after him."

"You know what?" Tyler says. "We should give each other nicknames!"

"Yeah," they all agree.

"We got Vangogh," Tyler states. "Schuyler loves flying, so we can call her Sky. Charles, you like gold chains... So let's call you 'Chainy.' Matthias, you got mad fightin' skills—even if you can't beat your pops yet. So, you're MMA after those mixed martial arts fighters."

"You guys can call me Glock," Cory interjects. "I like guns."

"And Mercedes…" Tyler thinks, "Well, you're already named after a car."

The group laughs.

"I know," she replies, "but what about, Mary J?"

"Like after Mary J. Blige?" He balks. "You can't sing!"

"I can too!" She giggles.

"No you can't," everyone declares in unison.

"Ok, what about me?" Tyler questions. "What's my nickname?"

"How about Big Mouth?" Schuyler quips.

The group laughs.

"You like always talking," Chainy states. "We can call you… Sir Talks A Lot."

"I like it," Tyler smiles.

"Hey Vangogh," Sky interjects, "can you draw me a cool picture of a bird flying?"

Chapter Three

EXPERTS DON'T KNOW EVERYTHING

"The experts said airplanes couldn't break the speed of sound. And then the experts were proven wrong." - Anonymous

Schuyler sits in front of her guidance counselor for the first time. It's the first day of 9th grade and she doesn't want to waste any opportunity to make the school year as productive as possible. Mr. McTanner, a white man with a tall and lanky frame, looks through her transcript from middle school.

"These are some pretty decent grades for someone with your background."

"Thank you."

"I usually have to chase students down to meet with me. But you seem to have some initiative."

"Yes. I need to do well and I don't have time to waste."

"So, you have an idea of what you want to do with your life?"

"Yep! I love anything that flies! I want to become an aerospace engineer and figure out how to make a human fly in the air like a bird."

"That's... pretty specific."

"Yes. And—"

"*And* I also think that is a bit too unrealistic for you," Mr. McTanner frowns sympathetically.

"What do you mean?"

"Well, to be an engineer of *any* kind you would have to take a number of different types of math and science classes, like Trigonometry, Calculus and Physics—which comes after Earth Science, Biology and Chemistry. That can be grueling, even for the smartest of kids. And then, there's the difficult path of getting into a good college or university with a good engineering program. They are *extremely* competitive. And the workload can be so heavy, that people drop out or switch to a different area of study. Look, you've just started the first day of ninth grade. You have plenty of time to explore other options and figure out what to do with your life. Maybe even start with a 2-year community college if you graduate from high school."

"You mean, *after* I graduate from high school."

"Yes," Mr. McTanner smiles uncomfortably, "I meant *after* you graduate." He stands up and motions for her to walk with him to his door. "I just want you to try and enjoy the experience of school. Go to class. Make friends. Have fun! Don't stress yourself out before you begin. And I will do my best to make sure you are on track for a bright future *after* you graduate from high school."

Later that night...

Schuyler, Tyler and their dad sit at the kitchen table eating dinner.

"So, how was the first day of high school?"

"It was alright," Tyler replies while stuffing a forkful of food into his mouth.

"And what about you, Sky?"

"My day was good," Schuyler replies with a hint of hesitance. "I met my guidance counselor this morning."

"Great. How do you like him? Is it a him?"

"Yes. Mr. McTanner. He asked me what I wanted to be and I told him. Then he... *nicely* told me that I should consider being something *other* than an aerospace engineer."

"He said what?" Jacob yells.

"He said there were a lot of hard requirements to become an engineer. And even the smartest kids have problems making it."

"Well, he is your guidance counselor," Tyler replies. "Sounds like he's looking out for you. Give me the easy path any day! Wish he was *my* guidance counselor."

"No," Jacob barks. "He's not looking out for you, Schuyler. And the easy path isn't always the best path, Tyler."

"Here you go," Tyler interrupts, "you gonna tell me about all the benefits of hard work again."

"Son, you can't beat hard work."

"Well, look where it's gotten us."

"It's gotten us an apartment, food on the table and clothes on your back!"

"A broke down apartment with roaches," Tyler loudly counters. "And I wish we had better clothes and more food. Hard work is too hard. Easy is where it's at."

"What. So, now you want easy money? You want to sell drugs or rob someone to get your cash?"

"Guys on the block make more in a day than you probably make in a month."

"You need to stop hanging out with Cory."

"Why? He's my friend! He's Schuyler's friend too. We go way back!"

"That might be true, but he's changing… and not for the better. I see him hanging outside in the middle of the night when I'm on my shift."

"So. Maybe he just don't want to be upstairs! He's got a lot of people in his apartment?"

"And he's hanging out with *known* drug dealers. I don't like it. You need to distance yourself from him. Both of you do."

"Sometimes I wish—" Tyler bites his tongue.

"What?" Jacob retorts.

"Nothin." Tyler looks at the floor.

"Not nothing! Go ahead and say it! Sometimes you wish what? That you weren't my son?"

"… You said it."

"Well, if it wasn't for me, you'd be dead! You hear me?"

"Dad?" Schuyler interrupts. "What do you mean?"

Jacob gazes at his two children in silence. "I… I never told either of you because you were too young… and I probably shouldn't tell you now."

"Tell us what?" Tyler asks reluctantly.

"Your mother," Jacob hesitates. "I never told you the whole truth about why she's not here...After you both were born, she was diagnosed with Postpartum Depression. Sometimes it happens to mothers after they give birth. There are different levels to the depression, and it turned out your mom had the worst kind. Medication didn't seem to work. And on top of that there were *two* of you."

"What... what are you saying, Dad?" Schuyler asks.

He breathes heavily. "I'm saying... you were almost 6 months old... and your lives were in danger."

☊

Thirteen years earlier...

The elevator chimes on the 12th floor of the apartment building. The door squeaks open as an exhausted Jacob steps out in his full EMT uniform with his workbag hanging from his shoulder. The sound of babies crying pepper the hallway, but Jacob pays no attention to them as he shuffles down the hall towards his apartment. As he gets closer, he notices the sound of the crying grows louder. His heartbeat increases along with his stride as he sprints to the front door. He can hear *his* babies screaming.

Jacob quickly unlocks the door and bursts inside.

"Sheah!" He looks around quickly, but sees no one in the living room. "Sheah, where are you?" He drops his bag and jacket and runs to the kitchen and then to the bedroom. He sees his wife sitting on the edge of their bed, but the cries of his son and daughter are coming from the bathroom. Suddenly, another sound registers in his ears: running water.

He quickly opens the cracked bathroom door and enters to find Tyler and Schuyler lying in the tub, the water just starting to cover their faces.

"No!" He rushes over, snatches them from their ice-cold watery grave and lays them over his knee to make sure their airways are free from water. As he stands to his feet, he holds both of them in his strong arms and kisses them repeatedly. "It's okay... It's okay... Shhh... Daddy's here now... Daddy's here."

Their crying stops as he rushes into the bedroom, lays them in their cribs and wraps them in blankets. Jacob turns to his wife, who is slumped over sobbing—her eyes staring into empty space.

"What's wrong with you?" Jacob yells as he stands in front of his wife. "Sheah! You hear me talking to you?"

"I'm sorry!" She screams between her tears. "I'm sorry! I just couldn't take their crying anymore... Their crying was so loud and no matter what I did they wouldn't stop! I just wanted them to be quiet... I just wanted them to be... quiet."

ဂ

Back at the kitchen table...

The three of them sit silently around the table for several minutes. The only sound heard is the tic toc of the wall clock.

"I've been doing the hard work ever since." Jacob wipes his face. "I'm doing the best I can to make a place for you in this world. I expect the both of you to do the same. So, Tyler, don't talk to me about making easy money. That's an excuse for not living up

33

to your true potential. And Schuyler, don't listen to Mr. McTanner. You can be whatever you want to be if you are willing to put the time in and do the hard work. It appears I need to come to the school and switch you to a different guidance counselor."

⌒

Atlanta. The Present. Powersuit Technologies. Job Interview.

Curtis sits stunned by the story so far.

"Sounds like you have a wonderful dad."

"Yes. I do. Always in our corner."

Just then, his cell phone rings.

"I'm sorry," he says while looking at the display. "It's my wife." He takes the call and walks over to the corner of the room. "Hey honey. You alright? Yeah, I'm in a meeting. Yep. With the girl who did the flight video."

Schuyler tries to look like she's not listening as her attention drifts to the poster on the wall. She reads each line of the core philosophy of the company.

"Okay. Great," Curtis continues. "So, your brothers are coming in tonight. Sure. Go ahead and confirm the reservations for the restaurant. Yeah, Treyshawn is driving down with his mom and dad. Omar and mom are picking Mr. G up at the airport at 5pm. Yeah, it'll be great to get the team back together. Okay. Talk with you later. Love you. Bye." He comes back over to the table and sits down.

"I think it's great you and Kelly got married," Schuyler smiles.

34

"I do too," Curtis laughs. "Two and a half years and counting. But back to you. Where's your mother now? Do you have a relationship with her?"

"Yes. She came back around shortly after we started high school."

∩

December. 2014. Jacob's living room.

"Are you serious?" Tyler yells. "It doesn't take 14 years for someone to get their life right! I've got nothing to say to her!"

"She's your mother," Jacob huffs. "And she's ready to meet both of you."

"So, where's she been all these years? You think I want to spend my Christmas with someone who tried to murder us and then abandoned us?"

"I told you she was sick, Son."

"Well, I want to meet her," Schuyler replies sheepishly.

"You can't be for real!" Tyler contests.

"You don't think I've been mad?" Schuyler asks. "I've been mad too! But she's still... our mother. And if Dad thinks it's okay for her to come see us, then I'm willing to take the chance. It's not her I trust—at least not yet—it's Dad."

"So, what? Now we gonna be a family again?"

"No," Jacob replies firmly. "A lot of time has passed. And we are in very different places now. But she is still the woman who gave birth to both of you."

"I don't know," Tyler frets.

"It's only one night," Schuyler comforts.

"That's right," their father agrees. "This is only one night. And if you both don't feel comfortable after you meet her, then we don't move forward with any other encounters."

Tyler looks at his sister and father, weighing the options.

"You promise? *One* meeting?"

"*One* meeting," Jacob confirms, "And then we decide together if we will meet with her again."

☋

Christmas Day. 2014.

The buzzer rings as Schuyler, Tyler, their father and Aunt Takeisha scramble to finish straightening up the apartment. Jacob buzzes her in.

"Alright. We've got at least three minutes before she reaches us! Hurry!"

Another couple of minutes pass before they are ready. Good thing too, as the front door rattles with several knocks. Jacob slowly disengages the three locks and opens the door. He sees his ex-wife standing before him, looking more radiant than she did on their wedding day.

"Hi," she whispers with a smile.

"Hey," he replies. "Come on in." He steps back to make room for her entrance. His sister is the next person she sees.

"Hey Takeisha!" she smiles.

"Hello Sheah," Takeisha answers with a bit of hesitant skepticism.

It is then that she sees them.

"Schuyler... Tyler," Jacob declares warmly, "this is your mother. Sheah, these are your kids."

Sheah gazes at her son and daughter in silence as tears swell in her eyes. Schuyler and Tyler slowly look from their mother to each other and then back at her again. Sheah slowly raises her arms and smiles as she takes a step towards them.

"Schuyler. Tyler. It's good to finally see you again. It's been a very long time."

"It sure has," Tyler states flatly as he takes a step back. "Too long." He turns and walks away.

"Tyler!" Jacob yells. "Get back here!"

"No, it's okay," Sheah replies. "Don't force him."

"Mom," Schuyler utters as she takes several steps forward and hugs Sheah.

Mother and daughter stand and cry in each other's embrace.

"I'm so sorry," Sheah repeats over and over. "I should've come back to you both sooner."

"It's okay, Mom." Schuyler interrupts soothingly. "You are here now."

The night passes with Schuyler, Sheah, Jacob and Takeisha having great conversation over dinner. But Tyler, has isolated himself.

"That boy needs to come out of his room and be here with us," Jacob declares as he gets up from the table.

"Let him be," Sheah replies, "Give him time to process. I'm not mad. Sometimes, you can't force a boy or he'll push right back."

"Ain't that the truth," Takeisha quips.

The end of the night arrives and Sheah gathers her things as Jacob, Schuyler and Takeisha walk her to the door.

"Tyler!" Jacob calls. "Your mother's leaving now."

They all wait a moment, without any response from Tyler, before Jacob opens the front door.

"It was good to see you, Sheah."

"You too, Jacob." Sheah looks at her daughter. "Do you think we could do this again sometime?"

"I don't see why not," Schuyler smiles. "Maybe Tyler will be ready by then."

Sheah hugs everyone, walks out of the door and stops.

"Jacob?"

"Yeah."

"You're doing a great job with them."

"Thank you."

The door closes as Sheah walks down the hallway towards the elevator.

"Well," Jacob says to Takeisha and his daughter, "that went well."

Unknown to everyone, Tyler's door has been cracked open the entire time. He sits on the floor in his room with tears streaming down his cheeks. He's heard every word spoken that night, yet he still feels trapped in the past—unable to let his mother's transgression go. A minute passes before he gets up and walks over to the window. He looks down to the quad below and watches people enter and exit the building. He strains to see his mother leave and watches as she walks up the block and catches a bus that has just arrived.

Atlanta. The Present. Powersuit Technologies. Job Interview.

"So, how was it having your mother back in your life?" Curtis inquires.

"It was wonderful," Schuyler replies. "At first, we saw her once every other month, but eventually, we got to see her every other weekend. She became an important part of our lives again. Even though she and my dad didn't get back together, she was present at all of the important moments like birthdays and graduations."

"That's beautiful," Curtis smiles. "How did she feel about your dream of flight?"

"Oh, she embraced it fully!" Schuyler smiles at the thought. "I don't know if she really believed in the dream or if she knew she hadn't been around for most of my life, so she *better* believe in it... but she embraced my efforts to make it a reality. Over the years, when others said what I wanted to do couldn't be done, she always told me—just like my father—that anything was possible. I just needed to figure out how."

"Did your brother come to accept your mother?"

"It was a tough process, but he eventually came around. He can be a real hard-head most of the time."

"So, what happened with your 9th grade guidance counselor?"

"My dad came in and had a conversation with him," Schuyler laughs. "It went something like this… 'You keep your racist and classist thoughts to yourself. *Your job* is to advise these students towards greatness so they can make a positive difference in society! From this point on, if I *ever* find out you are discouraging my daughter from what she is capable of accomplishing you will have a big problem legally and physically.'"

"Wow!" Curtis exclaims. "What did your guidance counselor say?"

"I don't know," Schuyler chuckles, "But from that point on, he was always very eager to make sure I had the best classes and that I did my best. In fact, at my graduation, he thanked my dad for challenging him with the truth. He had spent so many years at the school, with decreasing resources and increasing negative interactions from other students and parents. He simply resigned to the belief that we weren't capable of anything other than mediocrity at best."

"But you proved him wrong."

"Yes. With my father's help, I did. You know, he's never stood in the way of anything I was truly passionate about. He's always used his connections and resources to help me achieve my goals. Really, if it wasn't for him, I might not have been able to reach this aspect of my dream."

Chapter Four

FLYING HIGH

"One can never consent to creep when one feels the impulse to soar." - Helen Keller

Sunlight swept into Schuyler's room on the morning of July 1st. It's only been several days since the last day of her 10th grade year. She awakes to find a birthday card sitting on her nightstand. She sits up with wildly matted hair; stretches long and hard before rubbing the cold from her eyes. A moment later, after a slow deep breath and a lazy gaze out of her sunlit window, she picks up the card and holds it in her hands.

The front of the white card has an image of a soaring eagle. She smiles at the sight and opens to the inside. Some kind of folded document falls out, but before she can read that, the inside of the card captures her attention. There, a quote is boldly printed: *"One can never consent to creep when one feels the impulse to soar."* The name underneath the quote is Helen Keller. At the bottom of the card is a description written in her father's handwriting: *Helen Keller was a woman who was blind and deaf and went on to speak and teach around the world.*

"That's cool," she whispers as she puts the card down and picks up the folded piece of paper. She unfolds the document and covers her mouth with a gasp. A green Post-it Note displays her favorite quote from Bessie Coleman: "You've never lived until you've flown." Underneath the green note is the flight information for an airplane ticket to Atlanta. She had never been on a plane before.

"Daddy!" She yells while catapulting out of bed and bolting out of her room. "Daddy! Where are you?"

"In the kitchen!" Jacob yells back.

Schuyler runs into the kitchen to find her father and brother sitting at the table. Jacob has a broad smile on his face. Tyler looks indifferent.

"Are you sending me to Atlanta?"

"For a couple of weeks," he smiles. "You leave tomorrow."

She jumps up and down repeatedly. "Are you serious?"

"Yes," Jacob laughs. "Figured your birthday would be a good time for you to fly down and visit some of our relatives."

"Thank you. Thank you! Thank you!!" She laughs while giving him a strong hug. "Are you going too?"

"No," Jacob frowns a bit. "Gotta work. Couldn't afford for all of us to go. Besides, Tyler has summer school."

"Awe man," Schuyler frowns.

"That's what I said," Tyler replies sarcastically.

"But there's more," Jacob continues. "Not only will you fly on a plane for the first time, but I spoke to Uncle Willie and he's arranged for you to take flying lessons while you're there."

"Wait! You mean I'll be able to *learn* how to *fly* a plane?"

"That's what I mean."

"Shut up!" She laughs. "This isn't happening!"

"Oh, it's happening, Sweetheart!" Jacob smiles.

"This is ridiculous!" She laughs again.

"Tell me about it," Tyler frowns as he abruptly scrapes his chair back, stands up and walks out of the room.

"Tyler!" Schuyler calls as she follows him. "Why are you upset?"

"Are you serious?" He snaps. "I can't believe you gotta ask! You get to go down South while I gotta stay here with Dad."

"It's not my fault you have summer school," Schuyler replies.

"Oh, so now it's *my* fault!"

Jacob stands in the doorway watching the exchange.

Schuyler looks at her brother with a softening expression. "I'm not pointing blame," she comforts. "We are where we are because of the choices we make. If you don't like it, then start making better choices. That's all."

"Easy for you to say," Tyler frowns. "You always got your head in them clouds... dreaming about stuff that ain't gonna happen."

Schuyler stops and looks at her brother while shaking her head. "What? Would you rather me stay here?"

Tyler gazes at his sister like she's got two heads.

"No, stupid! You better go to Atlanta. Dad already bought the tickets and got everything set up! Besides, I don't want him to be mad at me for stopping you!"

Schuyler's eyebrows wrinkle in confusion. "So, why are you mad?"

Tyler looks off for a moment before mumbling, "I don't know."

She smothers him with a huge bear hug. "You know I love you, right?"

"Yeah, yeah. Send me some pics of you flying in that plane."

LaGuardia Airport.

Schuyler sits in her seat with her face plastered to the window. Her cheek muscles grow tired from the immense grin on her face. She is like a kid in a toy store, full of glee so overwhelming that it spills over to the passengers sitting next to her.

"This is your first time on an airplane, huh?" A slightly overweight white man in his sixties with greying hair inquires.

"Oh, you could tell?" she beams sheepishly.

He laughs heartily and smiles back at her. "You've been staring out the window the entire time, giggling and we haven't even pulled back from the gate yet." He winks. "Just wait until we get in the air."

The plane's engines slowly roar to life as it backs away from the gate and taxis to the runway for takeoff. Schuyler sits back in her seat and eagerly watches the flight attendants as they demonstrate the safety features of the aircraft. Once complete, the captain's voice is heard over the intercom system, informing the passengers they are next in line for takeoff.

"Now this is where the fun *really* begins," the man smiles.

The plane's engines roar like a pack of lions as it suddenly lurches forward with a jolt and begins its trek down the runway. Schuyler lets out a gasp—slightly mixed with awe and nervousness.

With each passing second the plane and its passengers speed up! Schuyler can feel the front of the plane start to rise as she looks out the window just as it takes to the air! She lets out a scream of overwhelming joy which is heard clearly by all passengers on board. A wave of chuckles pepper the cabin as Schuyler covers her mouth with her hand, slightly embarrassed and sits back in her seat.

"Sorry!" She half whispers to her neighbor.

"Nothing to be sorry about," he chuckles. "Your excitement is refreshing."

For the rest of the flight, Schuyler never misses a moment as she sees for the first time, the clouds, blue sky and the ground from a completely different perspective.

"When you can fly," she whispers to herself with a child-like wonder, "...anything is possible."

☊

Atlanta International Airport.

Schuyler disembarks from her plane amidst of dizzying array of hugs and waves from the flight crew and other passengers. She waves goodbye and turns to look at the host of selfie pictures she just took with the captain and crew. *That was great!* She thinks to herself while making her way to baggage claim.

"Uncle Willie!!!" She screams as she sees him standing with her checked luggage in his hand. He's a well-dressed burly man with a well kept beard, short wavy haircut and custom wide framed orange glasses.

"Hey Sweet Pea," he shouts as he scoops her up into his arms and smothers her with the warmest hug he can muster. "The last time we saw each other, you were a little girl running around with your arms outstretched like bird wings. Look at you now. You are growing up into a fine young lady! How was your flight?"

"Absolutely amazing," she gushes!

"If you think that was nice," he smiles, "wait till tomorrow when your flight lessons begin!"

Schuyler jumps for joy repeatedly. "I can't wait!"

"Well, you have to!" Her uncle laughs. "Let's get you into the car. Your aunt is home fixing a nice meal for us."

"I can't wait to see Aunt Veenue."

"And she's looking forward to seeing you, too."

◑

Atlanta. Uncle Willie's House.

"You grow more beautiful every time we see you," Aunt Veenue declares as she lays eyes on her niece, who just walked into the kitchen. After a quick dry of her hands, she approaches with wide-stretched arms and embraces Schuyler. "The pictures your father sends don't do you justice."

"Aw…" Schuyler blushes as she hugs her aunt. "Thank you! And you look like you don't age!"

"I don't," Aunt Venue winks as she flares her long brown hair with a twirl. "64 never looked so good."

They both laugh as Uncle Willie interjects. "Schuyler, let me show you where you'll be sleeping. By the time we come back, it should be time to eat."

Minutes later they return to a dining room table full of food. The three talk into the night with much laughter.

◖

Atlanta. Airplane Flight School.

Early the next morning, Schuyler, Uncle Willie and Aunt Veenue arrive at the flight school. The air is crisp and the sky is clear— punctuated by beams of radiant sunlight. The hangar sits on the right side of the field. In front of it rests several parked Cessna airplanes. Some two seaters and others which seat as many as ten people.

"I can't believe I'm actually doing this," Schuyler mumbles to herself with a nervous excitement.

"Oh, you're doing it, alright," Uncle Willie utters with a sense of gratification as the owner of the flight school approaches. He's a tall, lanky black man with a wonderful smile.

"William! So good to see you!"

"Larry! Good to see you, too!"

"Is this the future pilot?"

"Yep!" Willie beams. "This is my niece, Schuyler."

"Well Schuyler," Larry declares, "since you are only in town for a couple of weeks, I've arranged for you to do a lot of your learning in the air. This way, you can get the most out of the experience."

"No way!" Schuyler claps. "Can this day get any more amazing!"

"Sure can," Larry laughs. "Let's get you ready to fly!"

The next hour is spent going through a flight checklist, followed by Schuyler and Larry taking their positions in the pilot and co-pilot seats. With the turn of a switch, the airplane's engine sputters to life as the propeller begins to spin—slowly at first, and then within seconds at full speed. With the pull of a lever and the release of the brake, the Cessna taxis across the tarmac to the runway. Once there, the pilot accelerates the plane down the airstrip and pulls back on the stick—sending the plane into the air. Within minutes, the plane reaches over 2,500 feet.

"So, what do you think of the view?" Larry yells into his headset microphone.

"What do I think?" Schuyler yells back over the roar of the engine. "This plane is really loud… and really cool!"

"I know. Sounds like we're stuck in a blender!" Larry smiles. "There's no feeling quite like it! I want you to take the controls."

A nervous Schuyler follows the command and watches as her instructor relinquishes his grip from his control wheel as she grasps the one in front of her.

"It's your plane now," Larry smiles as he looks at his new student.

"I can't believe I'm actually flying a plane!"

"Well, you are doing it."

"This is one of the best days of my life!" She laughs. "Can I land?"

"Mmmm," Larry considers, "That's probably not a good idea

just yet. I have plans tonight," he chuckles. "Taking off is much easier than landing."

"Will I be able to do it by the end of my classes?"

"I don't see why not. You seem to be a quick study. If you continue to show a growing aptitude for flight, doing your initial landing should be a breeze."

By the end of the two weeks, Schuyler has become as proficient as someone who's been taking lessons for several months.

"She's like a sponge," Larry shares with William as they both watch her finish up her post flight checklist. "Whatever I throw at her, she soaks it right up. I haven't met many people who learn like she does. She has the gift for flying."

"Thanks so much for all of your help," William responds.

"Well, you did pay the fee," Larry chuckles.

"Yes," William agrees, "but you went above and beyond."

"Anything for an old friend."

"Is that what we are? Old?"

Schuyler approaches after completing her final closeout procedures.

"Thank you so much for this," she beams. "It has been awesome!"

"You made it easy," Larry replies. "Next time you're in Atlanta, the lessons are on me."

"Really?"

"Really."

"Thank you!" Schuyler gives him a huge bear hug.

"I hope you go far with flight young lady. Don't believe anyone who tells you, you weren't made for this."

Atlanta. The Present. Powersuit Technologies. Job Interview.

"That must have been a great experience," Curtis comments.

"It was," Schuyler agrees. "It really was."

"How did it feel to fly the airplane for the first time?"

"Honestly?" Schuyler hesitates. "As great as it was, I felt like I was sitting in a big box that was flying. I felt... detached from the sky."

"I see. Was that when you knew you wanted to pursue other avenues of flight?"

"Yes. I just didn't know what those other avenues were. I still felt like I wanted to fly through the sky like a bird... just me and the wind—no metal box with wings."

"So, what did your dad and brother think about your adventure?"

"I'm not sure, actually. They were too busy dealing with a major issue so we never really got a chance to talk about it."

50

Schuyler and her father ride the bus back from the airport in silence.

"Dad? Don't you want to know how my trip went?"

"Mmm?"

"You seem distracted. What's wrong?"

"I don't know how to tell you this."

"Tell me what?"

"Your brother… is in jail."

"Jail?" Schuyler yells as people on the bus turn and look at her. She tries not to notice their stares. "I was only gone for two weeks," she whispers. "What happened?"

Tyler and Cory sit in a red sports car with tinted windows, parked across the street from a bodega: the corner store.

"You sure about this?" Tyler asks.

"I'll be in and out." Cory utters as he checks his gun. "Quick money. Been watching this guy for months. Owner always takes his big stash out at nine o'clock."

"And all I got to do is drive?"

"That's it," Cory smiles slyly. "Just keep the car running and wait for my signal." Cory steps out the car, with his gun tucked in his waistband and quickly crosses the street—looking both ways before entering the bodega.

Tyler's nervousness causes him to sweat profusely. He rolls the two front windows down to get some air.

A few minutes pass before the front door flies open and Cory runs out with two bags in hand. Tyler throws the car in 'drive' and speeds into the middle of the street. Cory opens the car door as the owner of the store runs out with his shotgun in hand. Three shots are fired as Cory stumbles into the car. The back side windows shatter as a bullet streaks through!

"Go! Go!! Go!!!" Cory yells as Tyler smashes the gas pedal to the floor. The sports car roars like a tiger as it accelerates down the street in a plume of smoke.

"We did it!" Tyler yells. "We did it!"

"Yeah," Cory winces, "we did it."

"Quick money!" Tyler declares.

"Quick money." Cory agrees as he places his hand on his side. That's when he notices the blood beginning to pour from his hoodie. "Man…"

"What?" Tyler asks.

"He shot me."

"You hit?"

"Yeah…"

"I gotta get you to the hospital!"

52

"No! No hospitals. Take me back to the crib. I'll get one of my guys to bandage me up."

A block away from their building, Cory passes out from the blood loss. As Tyler pulls up, he sees his father heading to his ambulance to start his shift.

"Dad!" He yells as he screeches to a halt and jumps out the car. "Dad! I need your help!"

"Tyler?" Jacob asks as he stares at his son. "Who's car is this?"

"I don't know, but you gotta help me. Cory's been shot!"

Jacob leaps into action and calls his partner over. Tyler watches helplessly as they pull Cory out of the car, put him in the ambulance, cut away his hoodie and immediately get to work trying to save his life. The ambulance speeds off to the nearest hospital, leaving Tyler standing motionless in its wake.

Schuyler sits quietly, listening to her father recount the event.

"Cory didn't make it," Jacob declares. "And then later that night, the police showed up at the apartment. Turns out security camera footage showed Tyler as the driver for the getaway car. When they found and searched the car, they also found the money and a lot of drugs."

"So, the police arrested Tyler," Schuyler surmises. "That's how he ended up in jail."

Her father nods his head silently.

Atlanta. The Present. Powersuit Technologies. Job Interview.

"I'm sorry," Curtis shares. "That must have been tough."

"It was," Schuyler agrees. "And it just kind of overwhelmed everything I was doing. Tyler took precedence. And everything changed after that."

"How so?"

"My dad... he changed. He became less... optimistic. He was more anxious than usual."

"And what about your brother?"

"He had messed up his life, although he wasn't willing to admit it at first."

Chapter Five

OUR BIRTHRIGHT

"Flight is as much a choice as it is a birthright." - Anonymous

Schuyler sits at a row of desks separated by two partitions on each side. An intercom phone system hangs on one of them. A pane of glass sits dead center in front of the desk. On the other side of that glass is an almost mirror image, except the chair is empty. She nervously awaits the arrival of her brother as prison guards walk by amidst the buzzing of security locks and the clanging of closing gated doors. The cold surroundings of bolted down metal and security cameras is not inviting. It's not meant to be. Schuyler looks away from the sterility and loses herself in thoughts of flight in order to fight against her anxiety.

I believe we were all created to fly. That we have the capacity to rise above the gravity of our circumstances. We don't have to be bound to the surface of the earth if we don't want to be. Birds... Planes... Dragonflies... Helicopters... Gravity never ceases to exist for any of them. But there's another law at work which is also present, but primarily active only through a choice of will: The Law of Lift.

To access it is to choose. When certain conditions are met, a body that is heavier than air can rise against the force of gravity and soar through the clouds. But when the law is disregarded, gravity takes over again and we crash to the ground. Some of us choose not to fly for fear of crashing. We choose to merely... walk the earth. Yet, our choice does not negate the fact that we were still created to fly. Flight... is our birthright.

A gated door on the other side of the pane of glass buzzes open and Schuyler watches as a guard escorts her brother towards her. He is wearing what prisoners wear—an orange jumpsuit—and is shackled at his ankles and wrists. He plops down into the seat in a slouch and barely looks at her. She stares at Tyler intently. After a minute, he turns his attention in her direction. They look at each other in silence as she slowly raises her opened palm to the glass. But he does not reciprocate. She then reaches for the phone and places the receiver to her ear. He glares at her—almost as if he's staring right through her—caught in a gaze at something she can't see.

With a nod of her head and a raise of her eyebrow, she motions for him to pick up his phone. He sucks his teeth and glances sideways as he slowly reaches over, grabs the phone and places it to his ear.

"What you want?" Tyler mumbles sharply.

"I come to see you and you got an attitude?" Schuyler replies.

Her brother sucks his teeth again. "I ain't ask you to come."

"But I'm here," she states flatly. "And you didn't have to come out of your cell."

They stare at each other silently; neither one of them wanting to speak. Tears swell in Tyler's eyes as he sniffs them back with a sheer act of his will. Seeing his emotional fight, Schuyler's eyes swell with tears as well, but she lets them roll down her cheeks.

"Why did you have to go and do this?" She whispers.

"So, now you judging me?"

"No… I'm trying to understand."

"There's nothing to understand," he scoffs.

She stares at him while slightly shaking her head.

"Don't look at me like that," Tyler utters.

"Like what?" Schuyler questions.

"Like that! Like I'm an embarrassment to you."

"Why do you keep doing this?" She replies. "You are so smart—"

"Just shut up, okay? Just take your little dreams of flight and go somewhere else wit 'em."

"Is that what this is about? *My* dreams? *You* went and did something *stupid* because of my dreams?"

"What *I* did was stupid?" Tyler retorts. "What's *stupid* is *you* trying to chase a dream that will *never* come true!"

"So," she says while sitting back in her chair, "you're jealous."

"Jealous? I'm not jealous. You just need to get your head out them clouds."

"No. You're mad because I have a dream… and you don't."

Tyler just shakes his head as he looks at his sister. "You ain't got a clue, Sky. This is the *real* world we livin' in! And Cory's dead—"

"Don't try to hang this on Cory," Schuyler counters. "Yes, he's gone, but you made the decision to get in that car. You're always looking for ways to make easy money! When are you going to grow up?"

"You think you got it all figured out?" Tyler scoffs. "You really don't have a clue! You don't see how people laugh at you behind your back. How your 'friends' smile in your face and then call you stupid, dumb and wierd when you're not around. You know who has to deal with all of that? Me.

"You don't even know how long I've been defending you. How many times I had to tell people to back off because you weren't stupid. I'm tired Sky… I don't have the strength to do it anymore. I don't… have your strength to dream."

Schuyler gazes at her brother as tears flow freely down her face.

"First. I never asked you to fight my battles. People are going to say what they say. I'm not responsible for them, but I am responsible for me. Second. You've always told me my dream of flight was dumb. So, it's not just *other* people who's talking about me, but it's you too. So, don't try and act like the hero. You're just angry because I discovered my dream and you still don't have a clue about what you can do with your life!"

"So what if I don't know?" Tyler replies nonchalantly.

"Don't act like it doesn't bother you, Tyler. You made some bad choices and now you're stuck in here. You need to own your decisions so you can get free."

"It was supposed to be me!" Tyler yells. "*I'm* the oldest! I'm supposed to have it all figured out!"

"And then your little sister beat you to it. Don't forget you're only three minutes older than me," she quips.

"So? All eyes were supposed to be on me. Not you," Tyler admits. "And here I am, can't even make any of my plans work. Being a music producer and rapper didn't work. Nothing I try works. And here you come with your stupid dream, just plugging away at it everyday and it's working for you."

"Tyler, it was never a race between us—at least not on my end. You're my brother! I'm your sister! We're supposed to be on the same team. To be honest, I think the reason why your dreams don't work for you is because they are not *your* dreams. They belonged to your friends. They were ideas for getting rich so you could get out the 'hood.'"

"What else is there?" Tyler yells. "You think I like where we live? I hate it! All I want to do is get out as quickly as possible. And I'll take whatever route that gets me out the quickest. There's nothing else to dream about, Sky."

"There's *everything else* to dream about," Schuyler counters as she gazes into her brother's eyes. "What else is there? There is so much more! There's a whole world full of dreams that can take you places without you ever having to break the law, or kill somebody, or compromise the principles dad works so hard to instill in us. Principles like *hard work, creativity, ingenuity, loyalty.* I don't like where we live either. But it's all we've got until we can move some place else. Trying to make *easy money* is a shortcut to a dead end street. You are better than this, Ty.

"And I don't know where my dream will take me. I don't know if I will ever fly in the way I truly hope to do one day. Sometimes I feel like my dream is crazy! But I can't get rid of it. No matter how hard I try, my dream of flight won't go away. It keeps me up at night. It captures my attention during the day. It's like this dream was crafted just for me. I don't know where it came from, but when I don't pursue it, I feel like I can't breathe.

"So, whether I fail or succeed, I have to see how this ends. Whether people are with me or against me, I have to try this with everything I've got! I *hear* what they say about me. But they don't have to *live* with me. *I'm* the one who has to look myself in the mirror every day. And you... you have to look at yourself in the mirror, too."

Tyler stares at his sister, unsure of what to say.

"I love you," she smiles while wiping tears from her eyes. "You are good at so many things! Maybe what you are supposed to do in life has to do with those things. Or maybe the dream that's for you will have to do with a skill and talent you haven't even discovered yet. I don't know… But don't let jealousy cause you to ruin your life. You are *absolutely* better than that. You are stronger than that. I know you can fly. Flight is as much your choice as it is your birthright. But if you don't free yourself from this bitterness, even if you get out of here, you will still be in a prison."

Once again, Schuyler places her hand on the window pane. This time, Tyler slowly raises his arm and presses his hand firmly on the glass. They both gaze into each other's eyes as the buzzer sounds and the guard arrives to take Tyler back to his cell.

Ω

Atlanta. The Present. Powersuit Technologies. Job Interview.

"So, what happened with your brother?" Curtis questions.

"He cooperated with the authorities. And I wrote a letter to the judge. My dad got several people to speak on his behalf, promising to help him turn his life around. He agreed he wanted to do better. And since this was his first offense, his charges were reduced and he was given community service if he agreed to join a community mentoring program that was specifically designed to help black boys."

"That… is an example of the justice system and the community working together. I love it! Where is your brother now?"

"Finishing up his senior year in high school. His bad grades caused him to be left back, but he is working hard to catch up."

"You know, your brother kind of reminds me of my friend Treyshawn. He had a rough start in life, and got left back too. But he was able to turn things around with some help and a deep change to his mindset. I'm glad your brother is doing better."

"Me too," Schuyler chuckles. "My dad is happy as well."

"I'm sure he is," Curtis agrees. "So, tell me more about your flight journey. If you felt like flying in an airplane was more like being in a 'box that was flying,' how did you make the transition to your invention?"

"I love this part," Schuyler beams. "A few days after I returned from Atlanta, I happened to overhear some people talking about this place called iFly Westchester. It's a vertical wind tunnel that had recently opened up in Yonkers. I had no idea what it was, but when they said you could fly just as if you were jumping out of a plane, but without the parachute, I knew I had to check it out."

☊

New York. July 18, 2016.

Schuyler registered for her visit right away. She had used some of her saved allowance to pay for her first flight at iFly Westchester. The trek from Brownsville, Brooklyn to Yonkers took approximately two hours and thirty minutes by public transportation—and that was just one-way. The trip consisted of her walking to the train station from her apartment; then taking two trains to the Bronx to catch a bus. She took the bus to the stop closest to iFly Westchester. Then she walked for thirty-six minutes, up and over a steep incline and past the Ridge Hill Mall, to get to her destination: the blue and grey colored iFly building.

By the time she arrived, her body was hot, tired and sweaty. But she was determined to experience what was certain to be a unique event—one she hoped would be both exhilarating and eye opening about the dynamics of human flight. This was going to be the closest she had ever been to her dream of human-free-flight. Her mission was two-fold: to have fun and to learn how the tunnel worked. She had binge-watched all of the vertical wind tunnel videos she could find on Youtube. She was familiar with the terminology and had even practiced the basic aerial body positions on her bed. She was as ready as she was going to be.

She stood in front of the building's double doors, listening to the sound of multiple fans on its top, pulling air inside the structure. The moment felt electric, as if this was meant to be the next piece of the puzzle that constructed her dream of flight. *Am I walking into a key part of my destiny?* She thought to herself as she reached for the door's handle and began to pull. She was about to find out.

"Hello! Welcome to iFly Westchester!" declared a woman standing behind the front counter. Her tone was extremely chipper as she asked, "Do you have a reservation with us today?"

"Yes, I do," Schuyler replied with a huge grin. "This is my first time."

"Well congratulations," the woman smiled. "I am sure you will have a wonderful time today!"

After a few minutes checking in, she turned to enter the

observation lounge area and was immediately struck by the view. In the center of a dimly lit circular room sat a wide transparent, brightly lit tube stretching from the floor all the way up to a very high ceiling. In the center of this tube was a man hovering in mid air, wearing a red jumpsuit and blue helmet. Schuyler walked straightway to the vertical tube and stood in awe as the instructor demonstrated the basics of human free-fall to a group of awaiting visitors sitting in a side chamber connected to the tunnel. They were wearing jumpsuits and helmets of their own.

Schuyler understood the concept. After all, she had watched all of the videos she could find. But to see a person right in front of her eyes hover on a fast moving stream of invisible air was entirely more moving than any video. She slowly raised her hand and placed it on the transparent wall. It was cool to the touch and vibrated as the air rushed within the chamber.

As if on cue by an unseen director, the instructor spun in Schuyler's direction. When he saw her expression of child-like wonder, he smiled, waved at her and pointed up to the ceiling. She gazed up and then back down to him. Then he did something that took her breath away: with a three-count of his fingers he shot up to the top of the wind tunnel like a rocket, spun around in several flips and then zoomed right down to her again—stopping mere inches from the wall in a horizontal position. He then flipped upright and stood on the air with his arms out at ninety degree angles—perfectly vertical and "walked" to the doorway exit, landing with the grace of a majestic bird.

Schuyler made no waste of time running over to the equipment counter to get her flight gear. But first came her pre-flight training class. She sat in a classroom with several other people waiting to fly as an instructor walked them through the entire process and answered all of their questions. Now, it was time to get suited up!

Within minutes, Schuyler was clad in her own red jumpsuit, holding a red helmet as well. And the entire class filed into a waiting chamber, which was connected directly to the wind tunnel. One by one the instructor took each person into the tunnel for an individual lesson. Schuyler watched anxiously at each person, studying every move while trying to keep her excitement and impatience under control. Finally, the instructor motioned for her to enter. And as the wind raced upward in a controlled stream, she stepped into the airflow and found herself… weightless.

This… was a feeling like she had never experienced before! And her excitement was so intense she felt as if her heart was about to burst through her chest. She couldn't hear her instructor, due to the sound of the rushing wind, but she followed the prescribed hand signals which were given to help her correct her form. She was flying. She was also working quite a bit to keep her body at ease within the airflow. The wind wasn't exactly calm as this was not like floating in zero gravity, but as she started to relax *into* the airflow as it buffeted her body, the time for her first attempt was completed and the instructor led her to the doorway exit.

Schuyler landed with a shout of jubilation and as she took her seat, she watched the other students fly again. Then it was her time once more. As before, she yielded to the flow of the airstream and was airborne for a second time. The experience was just as amazing as the first one—with one difference. This time, the instructor grabbed onto the built-in handles on Schuyler's bodysuit and directed her. They both rose into the air and spun around; they hovered together and zoomed back and forth. Within the last thirty seconds, the instructor flew Schuyler almost to the top of the tunnel and brought her back down with a spin.

Then with only seconds left before her flight was to end,

the instructor released her to see if she could remember how to move towards the door on her own. Schuyler immediately positioned her body in the appropriate pose. Her legs extended back and her arms were out-but-tucked close to her sides. She flew forward to the doorway, where she grabbed both sides of the exit, tucked her legs and pulled herself out of the airflow. She landed with a shout as the other students and the instructor clapped for her. Her first free fall flight experience was complete. She was already eager for more. Flight was her birthright, and she was determined to claim what was rightfully hers.

Chapter Six
THE COST OF FLIGHT

"Flying might not be all plain sailing, but the fun of it is worth the price." - Amelia Earhart

Weeks pass as Schuyler treks back and forth from Brooklyn to Yonkers. Ever since that first flight, everything in her life began to change—starting with her new job. To her surprise, after she finished her first vertical wind-tunnel experience, she was preparing to leave the premises, when she noticed a bulletin board which listed a series of job openings which were available. She applied for the Guest Intake Receptionist position and got it! Now, thanks to her new job, she worked at the Tunnel five days a week and flew in the Tunnel during her off time—at a discount. But she didn't just fly in the Tunnel... she analyzed the physics of her flights and asked every question that popped into her head about how the entire tunnel operated.

By the end of the summer, she had a thorough understanding of the inner workings of the Tunnel and of the body mechanics that allowed her to move through the rising column of air with increasing grace and power. She took to Tunnel flying like a bird takes to the air, and her rapid progress did not go unnoticed. By the beginning of September, thanks to a sponsor, she entered her first tournament competition on Labor Day. She came in third place. Considering she had only been flying for just over a month... needless to say people took notice. Yet, there was still this nagging thought in the back of her mind...

What will this dream of flight cost me? Schuyler thought one day as she watched others fly in the Tunnel during her lunch break. As excited as she was, there was a silent sadness developing within her. As she watched a young boy—with a full smile on his face— fly for the first time, she uttered the words: "I'm still not free."

Schulyer was content, but not satisfied. "The vertical wind tunnel is not the fruition of my dream," she continued as she rose from the viewing couch and walked back to her position. "I can only fly in this tunnel. Outside of it, I am gravity-bound just like everyone else. And no matter how large the tunnel is—no matter how transparent the glass—it is still just like the plane… a box."

Once school began, Schuyler only worked at the vertical wind tunnel on weekends. Yet, each time she went to work, she wrestled with the question: *Is this box big enough for me?* But she already knew the answer. Now, she had to determine what she was going to *do* with her answer. *How much will this dream cost me? Both now and in the long run? Am I willing to pay that price? What if I give myself completely to this dream and pursue it with everything I've got and fail miserably? What if people laugh at me? But, what if I succeed? Isn't that possibility worth the trouble of finding out?*

Atlanta. The Present. Powersuit Technologies. Job Interview.

"So, was the vertical wind tunnel the closest you came to your dream before creating the wing-cape?"

"No," Schuyler smiles widely. "The closest was when my dad took me and my brother on a trip upstate to a hang gliding shop. It was at an airfield in Middletown, about two hours from home."

A rental car drives up the New York State Thruway...

"Dad, where in the world are we going?" Schuyler pleads from the back seat.

"That's the twentieth time you've asked," her dad laughs. "I'm still not telling you."

"Whatever it is," Tyler interjects—also from the back seat, "it better not be boring!"

"It won't be boring," Aunt Takeisha replies from the front passenger seat. "Both of you stop whining. We're almost there."

"You've never rented a car for us before," Schuyler utters.

"This is a special treat," her aunt replies.

"So, you DO know where we are going!"

"I'm not telling you either," Aunt Takeisha laughs.

Twenty minutes later, Schuyler's face and hands are glued to the window as they drive past the entrance. A large sign reads, 'Hang Gliding Classes.'

"No way!" Schuyler screams. "Are you kidding me?"

"This is an early birthday present," her dad declares with a twinkle in his eyes. "I know you love flying in the vertical wind tunnel, but once you said you still felt confined, I started looking around. This is about as close as you can get to flying like a bird."

"Your dad and I have been saving up so you could do this," Aunt Takeisha adds. "So, *both* of you could do this."

"Are you crazy?" Tyler balks as the car comes to a stop and they all exit the vehicle. "I ain't doing this! Black folk supposed to keep their feet on the ground!"

"Not true," his dad replies. "Black people have been involved in aviation for years. Don't be so limited." He smiles at his son. "You should do it."

"I ain't doing it," Tyler huffs as he crosses his arms tightly. "And you can't make me."

"Fine," his dad replies. "It's your loss."

They all walk over to the hangar and check in at the office. A few minutes later, Schuyler's training begins. For thirty minutes her instructor explains every facet of the brightly colored hang glider which sits before them. She eagerly asks a plethora of questions in response.

"We're going to do a tandem flight," the instructor concludes. "I am the pilot. You'll be along for the ride."

The training ends as she and her instructor suit up in all of the appropriate gear. They make their way outside to the airstrip where a hang glider sits ready to go. Jacob, Takeisha and Tyler follow as Jacob records everything with his phone.

"Can I go sit in the car?" Tyler sulks.

"No." Jacob replies. "I want you to see this."

"It's always about Schuyler and *her* dreams." Tyler mumbles.

Jacob turns and stares at his son. "That's not true," he counters.

"You never do this for *me*?" Tyler objects.

"I *am* doing this for *you*," his dad replies sternly. "For both of you. But you don't want to participate. It may be her dream, but you can benefit from it too."

"I ain't got no interest in flying." Tyler sucks his teeth.

Jacob turns off his phone and addresses his son directly. "Tyler, you don't have any real interest in *anything*. You just do what your friends do. And most of the time that involves *you* getting into trouble."

Tyler glares at his father in silence.

"I love you, Son. But you are wasting your life. And you've shot down everything I've presented to you over the years. So, what am I supposed to do?"

Tears begin to swell up in Tyler's eyes. But he says nothing as his father continues.

"The moment you find a dream that's *yours* is the moment I will back you in it one hundred percent. Come on... it's not too late for you to take the flight. The view at 2,500 feet might help give you a different perspective on life."

Tyler stares at his dad and then looks over at his aunt and sister. Schuyler is fully strapped into the hang glider as the instructor and assitant attach the tow line to the small airplane that will take them up into the sky. Takeisha smiles as she takes pictures.

"I'll just watch from here," Tyler responds as he steps back a few paces.

"Dad!" Schuyler yells with a bright smile. "We're ready!"

Jacob turns his attention back to his daughter as they all watch the small plane accelerate down the runway with the glider in tow behind it. A few seconds later, both the plane and the hang glider are in the air, rapidly climbing to the desired altitude. A few moments later, the instructor disconnects the tow line and veers away towards a nearby hillside to catch an updraft. Within minutes, he and Schuyler are 2,500 feet in the air—soaring like an eagle. Schuyler is all smiles as her arms are outstretched like bird wings.

For twenty minutes they traverse the country-side while doing a series of turns, dips and climbs. And then, just as effortlessly as they took off, they land. Once they unstrap from the glider, Schuyler's exuberance breaks forth.

"THAT WAS AMAZING!" she declares at the top of her lungs while hugging her instructor repeatedly. "THANK YOU!"

Schuyler runs over and hugs her dad and aunt. "Thank you for this wonderful experience!"

𝍖

Atlanta. The Present. Powersuit Technologies. Job Interview.

"That is great! Man, your dad should get an award! So, how did that make you feel?"

"I loved it," Schuyler breathes deeply, "Immediately, I thought it was the fulfilment of the dream. I was ready to take up hang gliding! We were talking non-stop on the way back home. But then everyone got quiet. I guess we ran out of things to say. That was when I started thinking, *as great as it was, I was still... strapped into this pouch, which was attached to this large wing above me.* And there was this big metal bar you had to hold in order to shift your weight to change direction.

"Yes, I was freer than I had ever been—and it was glorious— but I still felt like I was connected to a large machine. It was flying and I was just along for the ride. I wanted it to be enough, but I just kept feeling like there was something more I was supposed to explore.

"So," Schuyler utters, "that's when I decided to truly pursue my purpose. I started analyzing everything about flight I had learned so far. I also studied everything I could find on hang gliders. Then I discovered skydivers who use wing-suits to fly for several minutes at a time. Shortly after that, I came up with the idea for my invention."

Curtis looks at Schuyler from across the table, unable to hide the fact that he has been hanging onto her every word. "Okay, by now you must have figured out that you got the job."

"I do?" Schuyler exclaims.

"Yep!" Curtis laughs. "No need to keep that bit of information from you any longer. Although I do want to hear the rest of your story at some point. Welcome to the team."

"Thank you so much," Schuyler beams as she reaches over the table and shakes Curtis' hand profusely. "When did you know?"

"I was already pretty sure. I just wanted to meet with you in person to *make* sure."

"And you're sure?"

"Yes. I am sure. Do you have any burning questions you'd like to ask me before we end?"

Schuyler's eyes dart back to the poster on the wall. "Actually... I read your company's core philosophy..."

"Okay," Curtis replies with a raised eyebrow.

"I noticed that you have a Bible verse listed with each core belief." She hesitates for a moment. "I... never pegged you as being a religious guy."

"If by 'religious' you mean, allowing my belief in God to dictate how I view myself, how I treat others, and how I make decisions, then yeah," Curtis answers. "I'm guilty as charged. But, it's really *not* about being religious. It's about having a genuine relationship with Jesus Christ. And *that* relationship changes everything."

"So, with everything you've been able to accomplish," Schuyler hesitates a bit, "you're saying that in the end you attribute your success to God?"

Curtis stares at Schuyler with a smile. "Do you want my honest answer?"

"Absolutely!" Schuyler smiles slightly.

"I don't talk about it much, unless someone asks, but I honestly believe my relationship with Jesus is the most important factor in my success."

She looks at him almost dumbfounded. "Well... okay... why do you say that?"

"People say I'm really smart. And I've got the test scores to prove it. But, I've been in some situations that were *way* beyond me. And every time I've needed help, God has always been there to work things out. So, it doesn't matter that I'm a prodigy. Jesus knows everything and promises to be with me in every situation. And a person can't truly run *or fly* in life without him."

"You really believe that?" Schuyler shuffles in her chair.

"I do." Curtis can tell she's a bit uncomfortable. "Listen. I am a Christian. And I run my company by biblical principles. But everyone who works here is not Christian. In fact, we have some professed athiests in our ranks who are proud to be a part of the work we do.

"My goal is not to proselytize everyone. I'm just being true to the fact that my faith is a huge part of who I am—actually, it's the most important part of me. And when my staff or employees have questions about my belief in God, I answer them to the best of my ability. The bottom line for me, is to try and treat people like I want to be treated. And that's with love, respect and encouragement so they can become their best."

Schuyler sits quietly for a moment as her eyes catch the core principles poster again. Curtis interrupts the silence.

"The job is yours. But, if you want to take a day to think it over and decide if you really want it now, I'm fine with that."

Schuyler smiles. "I truly appreciate your sensitivity to how I might be feeling. It's just that this part of the conversation was unexpected. I don't go to church much. When I was little, my dad would take my brother and me on Christmas and Easter. But that was about it. We kind of grew out of going as we got older. My dad still prays over his food though. I've prayed a few times, but I really can't say God has been active in my life."

Curtis smiles broadly as he looks across the table at Schuyler. "Who do you think gave you the dream of flight?"

"You think God gave it to me?" Schuyler balks.

"You told me it felt like an invisible hand placed the dream in your heart when you were little. I call these 'deep dreams.' You just can't get rid of them, no matter what you do. I believe God gives them to us as a part of our purpose. And we must decide either to seek their fulfilment or seek to smother them under layers of life's concerns and distractions."

"I... never thought about it like that."

"From everything you shared with me today and what you've demonstrated so far, I'd say God has been pretty active in your life. But listen, take a day to think about this."

"Are you crazy," Schuyler chuckles with her eyes wide open. "I still believe working for you is the chance of a lifetime! No extra thought is necessary. I want this job!"

"Great! Welcome to the team—again." Curtis' watch buzzes. "I hate to cut our conversation short, but I have another appointment in fifteen minutes."

"So, what now?"

"Now, I will have you meet with my Human Resources personnel so you can fill out all of the pertinent paperwork. Your start date is Monday of next week. Then we can talk in detail about your wing-cape invention. I want to help you increase its lifting efficiency and maneuverability. Does that sound good?"

"Absolutely!"

"As I said before, I think your invention has great potential. And if you came up with that all by yourself, I can't wait to see what you can come up with if we work together."

"Thank you, Curtis. You've given me a lot to think about. I won't let you down! I do have one request, though."

"What's that?"

"Can you give me a tour of your Powersuits? I've always wanted to see them up close."

Schuyler leaves her new place of employment feeling as if she's on top of the world! Once in her car, she jubilantly shouts. Then she calls her parents and engages in an active conversation— recounting the entire day. To those walking by her car, her animated conversation appears quite humorous.

◯

Monday morning. January 14, 2019

Schuyler eagerly arrives early to her new job… like one-and-a-half hours early. Her glee runs over as she sees a sign at a parking spot near the front entrance. It reads, WELCOME SCHUYLER WATKINS! She parks and gets out of her blue and white Smart car with a cardboard box of items and a book bag over her shoulder. As she heads into the building, she stops and takes a selfie standing next to the sign.

She uses her employee ID card to enter the building and makes small talk with the receptionist before heading upstairs to her new office. Her name rests on the door. She slowly enters and places her belongings down on the floor. Her fingers skim the desk as she walks around it to sit in her chair. She's all smiles for a moment before going back to her box.

Within minutes, she takes each item and places them around the room. Her Helen Keller birthday card. Her favorite paper airplane. A model of a dragonfly. A golf ball. And a large picture of her hovering in a vertical wind tunnel. Just as she finishes decorating the space, Curtis walks by and stops.

"You're here early!" he smiles.

"I didn't sleep much," Schuyler beams. "Couldn't wait to get here."

"Did you like your welcome sign?" Curtis smiles.

"Yes!" Schuyler exclaims. "Thank you!"

"That's your spot for the first two weeks. Enjoy being able to park near the entrance. Since you're here," Curtis motions to the door, "let's get some coffee from the lounge and head down to the vault."

Powersuit Technologies. Basement.

The elevator doors open as Curtis and Schuyler disembark and walk down a long hallway. Several doors are scattered on either side of the hall. A rather large door sits at the end of the path. A number of cameras are visibly located along its perimeter.

"This is the vault," Curtis smiles as he places his hand on a sensor pad, followed by a retinal scan. "All of my company's major technological breakthroughs are housed inside here."

Multiple locks disengage as the large, thick door slowly opens. Schuyler follows Curtis as he enters the surprisingly large expanse as the room's lighting system activates. They walk past numerous stations—each with its own encasement and locks—until they reach the latter half of the vault. Here, another set of doors separate the front half of the vault from the rear half. Curtis places his palm on another sensor pad and does a retinal scan again. The first set of doors at the vault's entrance close, to Schuyler's surprise, as the second set in front of them begin to open.

Schuyler is speechless as the lights automatically flicker to life in this section, revealing thirteen suits standing in their individual holding cells.

"Wow..." she whispers with wide-eyed amazement. "They're all here."

"I know," Curtis smiles. "I still get giddy everytime I see them."

Schuyler walks over to the first suit. "So, this is the Mach-1 Speedsuit." She lightly places her hand on its blue and gold exterior. "The suit that started it all."

"Yep," Curtis agrees. "That's acutally the third upgraded version. But it's still pretty old school compared to the one I use now." He points to the next holding cell.

Schuyler barely breathes as she sees the second powersuit. "Is that the Mach-2?" she exclaims while running over to it. "This is the one that Chasm Montgomery made for you!"

"That's the one," Curtis smiles. "It's *way* more technologically advanced. I can run almost twice as fast in *that* than I can in the Mach-1. It also has a jet-assisted jump capability, which provides additional bursts of thrust, for a maximum of 30 seconds at a time. With it, a user can jump for a distance of 2-3 blocks."

Schuyler takes a closer look at the thrusters on the back of the suit. "Wow! That's cool. Why does it only last for 30 seconds?"

"It works like an afterburner on a fighterjet or a turbocharger on a muscle car. But instead of using up a lot of extra fuel, it uses extra electricity from the suit's power cells to run the jets at a higher rpm in order to draw in a much larger amount of air for thrust."

"That's a mouthful," Schuyler chuckles.

"It is," Curtis agrees. "Since those power cells run the rest of the suit's systems, 30 second bursts are the safety limit before the power drain becomes too much."

"I see," Schuyler nodds while making some mental calculations. "That's not bad."

"Thanks," Curtis replies. "The suit is pretty cool. I really enjoy the Mach-1, but I'm not going to lie... The Mach-2 is on a whole other level! And it takes longer for fatigue to set in because the suit reduces the physical stress to my body by a huge percentage... much more than the Mach-1. I really feel like I'm a passenger going along for the ride."

She gazes around the room at all of the familiar suits—each with its own unique capability: speed, sonics, electricity, acrobatics, fire, light bursts, strength augmentation, wall surface adhesion, camouflage, wind manipulation, kinetic redistribution—her gaze suddenly stops as she takes notice of a new addition. "You have been busy!"

"I have," Curtis agrees. "I spend a lot of time making upgrades to the 12 original suits, but I just recently finished a new aqua powersuit. The results of its range and manueverabilty in water look promising."

"So..." Schuyler utters with wrinkled eyebrows. "I've been to the museum that Mr. Montgomery had created about you. These suits are there, but they're here too?"

"The ones in the museum are mock-ups."

"Oh, good," Schuyler breathes. "So, if someone stole one..."

"Right," Curtis finishes her thought. "They don't work. All of the original and upgraded powersuits are housed right here under lock and key."

"Do you still use them?"

"On occasion," Curtis smiles. "Mostly for exhibitions, but sometimes for other adventures. Who knows. One day you might be able to be a part of the team that gets to use them."

"That would be amazing!" Schuyler can barely contain her excitement as she tries not to jump up and down.

"Well," Curtis motions towards the doors, "why don't we go to my workshop and take a look at your wing-cape design."

◯

Soon, they arrive in Curtis' workshop. He brings her video up on the wall's flat screen display and presses play. Schuyler appears—wearing a black padded jump suit and helmet—surrounded by her family and Mr. Larry, her flight instructor. The group stands at the top of a long grassy hill and help her strap into her flight harness—which is also black—and fasten the black wing-cape to its anchor points.

The task is completed a minute later as vocal commentary explains what she is about to do. Multiple cameras are seen at various points on the hill as she takes her place at the top. A countdown is given as she breathes heavily in anticipation. Then she runs to the hill's precipice and leaps into the air right at the point of the steep drop-off.

Everyone watches in awe as she glides quickly and safely down the hill—several feet above the ground—and lands at the bottom without incident. They all cheer as she breaks into a heart-felt laugh, as tears stream down her face.

Curtis watches the video with a broad smile as Schuyler opens her bag and places its contents on the table in front of them. Curtis turns to look. Before him sits all the elements of Schuyler's wing-cape invention.

"Is that what I think it is?"

"Yep! People have been asking how it works, but I haven't shared it, because I don't have a patent for it yet."

"Is that why the entire setup is black? To keep the parts hidden?"

"Yes. All the parts blend in with each other from a distance. You really have to be up-close and deliberate in your inspection to see the various components."

"That makes sense. Well, I can help you navigate the patent process if you like."

"Thank you! That would be a huge help! I trust you, so let me walk you through how the whole thing works."

For the next few moments, Schuyler shows Curtis the wing-cape and the harness it's attached to, while answering his intricate questions about its development and performance.

"You know, you never told me the whole story about how you came up with this idea."

"A couple of years ago I was browsing around on Youtube and discovered this guy named Yves Rossy."

"Jetman!"

"Yes!" Schuyler laughs. "That's him. When I saw him fly through the sky on his homemade wing, I knew that was what I wanted to do! I watched and analyzed every video I could find on him to try and understand how he was able to do what he did. In one video, he said when he was creating his wings, initially they were much larger. But then he realized he could use a smaller wing, if it was designed to be more efficient. But as much as I loved his wing design, I felt it was bulky. Functional... but bulky.

"I was already studying skydiving wingsuits, sports kites and kite surfing, as well as hang gliders and the Rogallo Wing created by Gertrude and Francis Rogallo back in the 1940's. After looking at all of these things, I realized I could use certain aspects from each design and combine them with my own ideas. That's how I came up with *my* iteration which is both a wing and a cape."

"Speaking of wingsuits... you know wingsuit flying is one of the most dangerous sports on the planet. People die while doing it every year."

"That's why I'm not jumping off of cliffs or out of airplanes. Only tall grassly hills for me right now. Although, my wing-cape has twice the surface area of a wingsuit. So, the glide ratio should be significantly better—if my math is right."

"That's good to know! I love how you reversed engineered seperate designs and came up with your own. Your story is the epitome of what it means to be a diligent innovator. It's like you're a detective, following the clues to see where they lead." Curtis rubs the wing-cape material between his fingers. "I see your wing-cape isn't made of regular fabric. It's very lightweight."

"Right," Schuyler agrees. "It's nylon, the same fabric that's used in wing-suits. The cape is a double layered cell design, equipped with ram inlets so air can fill the cape to give it the characteristics of a wing. It turns out my Aunt Takeisha is an excellent seamstress. She mostly makes dresses and suits. I didn't really think about what she did for a living until I had this idea. She agreed to help me. So, I got the material and gave her the design. She did all the measurements, created the patterns and sewed it all together. It took about eight different versions before we got it right."

"Wow. That's amazingly helpful to have an aunt who can sew!" Curtis exclaims. "I'm sure she saved you a lot of money." Curtis feels the material and notices some type of framework. "This seems to have some kind of internal skeletal structure."

"Yes. The internal structure of the wing-cape is made of sculpted foam infused with thin metal rods. It is only used on the top part where the cape attaches to the harness. The rest of the material fills with air to give it a level of fluid rigidity. The foam helps to add a definitive aerodynamic shape to the cape. And it provides the cape's anchor points for the cabling, which connects to my bodysuit's flight harness."

"A cable system? Now, that's ingenious."

"Thanks. I got that idea from researching how people use a cable system to change the direction of high performance kites and parachutes. Also, from my dad's ID badge which is connected to a spring-loaded cord which extends and retracts."

"It's amazing how you pulled inspiration from so many different aspects to put this invention together."

"I learned that from your story."

"I'm humbled, really. So, tell me more about the cable system."

"Right now, I just have three cords connected to the belt. They are cut to a pre-determined length, based on the flight characteristics I want, and attached to the cape by hooks. I'd love to get some more versatility out of the design by having some type of heavy duty spring-loaded system."

"That could work. The belt could have three spring-loaded pods connected to it. The cables could connect from those pods to the three main anchor points on the wing-cape. That way, when you run, the cape opens up in the wind and the cabling extends out under tension from the springs in each pod." Curtis continues to postulate.

"Or you could connect the wing-cape's cables to a series of winches on the harness. Then you can run a control line from the winches to your gloves. The winches default setting can allow the wing-cape to open fully for a sustained smooth forward glide. But by using the hand controls, you can retract or extend the cables to get a different wing shape. Like how a bird or a bat changes their wings' angle of attack or shape to turn, go faster, slower, etc…"

"That sounds like a great idea! Wow. You just came up with that on the spot?"

"That's how it happens sometimes," Curtis laughs. "But you provided the foundation for the idea."

"Thanks," Schuyler beams. "You know, I've always wanted to fly like a bird and this is the closest I've come… so far."

"So far?"

"Yes. I want to perfect this invention. I think it can be a great glider. But I also have two other ideas for powered personal human flight which I would like to pursue."

"Well… let's get to work seeing how we can make your wing-cape better. Then we can talk about your other inventions. And since you mentioned power… have you thought about adding some type of small jet to your harness? The propulsion could extend your flight time."

"I thought about it, but the fuel would add a lot of extra weight."

"Not if the jet is electric… like the Vortex Pack on my Speedsuit. The power cells are relatively light. I'll see what I can come up with."

"Sounds good to me!"

By the end of the day, Schuyler walks out to her car. Her body is tired, but her spirit is soaring. She gets in her vehicle and stares at the welcome sign. "I can't believe this is happening. This is a dream come true."

Her commute to and from work usually takes 25-30 minutes when she's rushing and there are no traffic issues. But today, she drives lazily home—too tired to rush—yet anticipating being able to collapse on the couch. Forty-five minutes later she shuffles through the front door of her 4th story apartment, drops her bag on the floor, and like the walking dead, makes her way over to the living room couch and crumbles into it with a groaning thud.

Her face is completely smothered by a pillow as her body slowly sinks into the cushions. Both her left arm and leg hang limp to the floor. A moment of silence passes without any movment before the muffled sound of her cell phone is heard. She grunts at the thought that her phone is in her bag which is on the floor by the kitchen. After four rings, the silence returns momentarily until the phone begins to ring again.

"Ugh!" She groans. "Go away!"

The phone stops ringing. A moment later, it rings again.

"Really?" She yells as she cranes her neck towards the bag. "Leave a message!"

The phone stops ringing. The silence returns until the phone rings again—this time with a FaceTime request ping. Schuyler forces herself to her feet, makes her way over to her bag and retrieves her phone. She's immediately alert when she looks at the display and quickly answers. Her dad appears on the screen.

"Dad!" Are you okay?"

"Hey Sky," he replies. "It's good to see my baby. Yes, I'm fine."

"If you're okay, then why did you call me three times?"

"Because I needed to speak with you. You look tired."

"I *am* tired," she huffs. "It's been a long day." Schuyler makes her way back to the living room and plops back down on the couch.

"Well, we can talk later if you want."

"Seriously? You call three times in less than five minutes and then say we can talk later?"

Jacob laughs. "I'm sorry about that..."

"So, what's up?"

"Well, I wanted you... to be the first to know," he declares with a mixture of reserved excitement and hesitation.

Schuyler's eyebrows wrinkle. "Know what?"

"Your mother and I... have been spending time together."

"Okay..." Schuyler replies nonchalantly. "You guys talk every week and mom visits at least twice a month to see us."

"No," her dad counters with a chuckle. "Your mother and I have been spending time... *together*."

Schuyler stares at her screen. "You mean like... *together— together?*"

"Yes," her dad laughs. "That's what I mean."

"Wha?" Schuyler is at a loss for words as she grapples with a flood of thoughts. "When? How? For how long?"

"I don't know how to explain it," Jacob rubs his hands through his hair with a sigh. "The last few weeks, we just started hanging out more. And then last night... we went out to eat... at that Chinese place you like downtown. Afterwards we were waiting for the train and... she kissed me."

"She did what?" Schuyler yells as she jumps to her feet. Her sudden jolt causes the phone to flip-flop out of her hand as she does a poor impression of a juggler in an effort to save the phone in midflight. She scrambles to pick the phone up from the floor while blurting out the five most important words she can think of. "So, what did *you* do?"

"Well..." her dad hesitates.

"Dad! Now is not the time to talk slow," Schuyler exclaims. "What did you do?"

"I kissed her back."

Schuyler's face explodes—at least she feels as if it does as her bulging eyes clearly reveals her shock to her father. She falls back onto the couch with the impact of a tree falling in the wilderness.

"Are you for real?" she whispers.

"Apparently," her dad laughs. "I was just as shocked as you when it happened."

"So, what are you going to do?"

"First, I want to know what you think," her dad replies seriously. "There's a lot of history here... and a major part of it isn't good. So, I need you to be honest with me."

"Well," Schuyler answers while trying to settle her thoughts and find her words. "She *has* changed a lot since she's been back in our lives. Personally, I'd love to see you two get back together. What do you think Tyler will say?"

"You know your brother can be unpredictable," her dad laughs. "But he has grown fond of her since she's been back in our lives. So, I imagine he will be open to the idea of your mother and I getting back together—if that's what we decide to do."

"Wow... my parents may be getting back together."

"For that to happen, you, me and your brother have to agree."

"Well, I for one, am all for it. If that's what you truly want. Honestly, don't just do it because she's our mother. If you get back together with her, do it because you love her and she loves you. Otherwise, you'll regret it."

"I hear you, Sky. And I appreciate the advice."

"Aw," Schuyler smiles as tears stream from her eyes. "I appreciate you, too! Really, I do!"

"I know you do," her dad smiles. "You have made me proud over the years. But... speaking of regret; I do have some not-so-great news."

"Oh, no," Schuyler inhales. "You can't give me great news and then follow it up with not-so-great news! I don't think I want to know what it is... Okay. Tell me."

"I ran into Mercedes the other day," he says sadly. "She just had another baby."

"Another baby?" Schuyler exclaims. "That's her third one! Is the father at least one of the *other* two guys?"

Jacob grows silent as he shakes his head. "No. I don't think so."

"I don't get it, Dad. Mercedes had so much potential. She could have been anything she wanted! But when she hooked up with the wrong crowd in 10th grade, she started changing."

"I know," her dad's voice trails off. "I did give her some money for diapers and milk."

"I'm sure she liked that."

"She was very grateful. You know, the next time you come up this way, maybe you can go see her."

"We haven't talked since 11th grade."

"I know, Sky."

"A lot has happened since then." Schuyler looks away. "A lot has happened to *all* of us."

"I know that, too," her dad agrees.

"Ever since Cory died..." Schuyler's eyes moisten as she fights to hold back tears. "We all just grew apart after that. I don't even know what we'd talk about. It's like they all just gave up on their dreams."

"Maybe you pursuing your dream can help them rediscover their own," her dad suggests. "Just... think about it, okay? You already know there's a cost to pursuing your dreams. And there's *also* a cost when we refuse to chase after them."

Chapter Seven
USING GRAVITY

"It is possible to fly without motors, but not without knowledge and skill. This I conceive to be fortunate, for man, by reason of his greater intellect, can more reasonably hope to equal birds in knowledge than to equal nature in the perfection of her machinery." - Wilber Wright

It's February 15, 2019. The sun crests over the pinnacle of a large mountainside. The air, on this Friday morning, is crisp, cool and flowing. Light puffy clouds accentuate the deep orange-blue sky as several birds of prey soar effortlessly across the firmament. At the juncture of the mountain, about half way down, a stream of orange cones create an 'S' pattern on the red dirt and sand all the way to the bottom plain. At this plateau stands a group of individuals preparing for something great.

Four weeks have passed as Schuyler has gotten acclimated to her new job. Her excitement brims over as she works directly with Curtis Powers on an assortment of projects. Even more so, Curtis has made his time available to help improve her wing-cape design with better materials and time spent flying in a wind tunnel. Now the day has come for them to test the upgraded suit.

The group of ten work feverishly to make sure all cameras

and testing equipment is set up to capture this experiment from all possible angles. The team triple-checks every aspect for accuracy as Curtis walks Schuyler through the new controls for the eighth time.

"Alright, repeat it back to me," he commands.

Schuyler effortlessly rattles off the information. "Winches are locked until I press the buckle release button. This keeps the wing-cape close to my side. Once unlocked, I use the hand controls to engage cable extension and retraction. Right hand turns me to the right. Left hand turns me to the left. Tilting hands down causes winches to retract the wing-cape for decreasing altitude. Tilting hands up causes winches to extend wing-cape to increase altitude."

"Good. Remember, this is about making small moves with your hands when the controls are engaged. If you retract too fast you'll plummet to the ground."

"Just one of the dangers of moving in three dimensions," Schuyler jokes.

"Yes," Curtis agrees with a half-hearted laugh, "please try not to crash. Remember, the new air-inlets should make for quicker airfoil inflation and if you need to bleed some air from the wing-cape, just squeeze the release pad built into the palm of your control glove."

"That's a long way down," Schuyler nervously chuckles as she gazes down the mountainside.

"You're the one who said, 'Go big or go home.'" Curtis laughs. "This site is a lot higher than the hill you did your initial flight on. That's why we upgraded your suit's padding. The material we used is more efficient at dispersing impact forces." Curtis hands Schuyler her helmet, smiles and walks over to an awaiting vehicle. "We'll see you at the bottom!"

Schuyler gives a nervous chuckle. "Hopefully in one piece."

The team takes their various positions as Schuyler stands alone at the edge of the cliff with her helmet in her hands. Only the sound of the wind is heard whipping by, punctuated by the echoes of distant birds.

She looks at the rising sun as its warm light shines across her face. She places her helmet on her head, secures its strap and takes a deep breath—slowly blowing it out through her lips. A voice squawks in her ear. "Ready when you are, Sky!"

"Copy," She replies. "Here we go…" She raises her right arm into the air, giving the team the signal to begin. Multiple cameras from various vantage points start recording. She backs away from the edge of the cliff by about thirty feet and presses the release buckle on her belt. The breeze captures her wing-cape as it begins to billow. A smile dances across her face as she listens to that sound and gazes at the open air in front of her.

Her muscles tense as she breaks into a run towards the edge of the cliff. The wing-cape expands, with the momentum of the moving air, and takes shape. Within seconds Schuyler screams at the top of her lungs as she leaps from the edge of the cliff— her eyes wide with a child-like anticipation. And then comes that moment of near weightlessness, when the wing-cape fully extends and the cables go taut as the fabric captures her body—as if a giant is reaching down to pick her up with his hands. She descends with increasing speed parallel with the mountain. With each passing second, the distance between the red earth and her feet grows: Six feet… Eight feet… Ten feet… Fifteen feet…

She glides on a downward trajectory—defying gravity's pull—

actually using it to her advantage—as she weaves to the right and left in a controlled descent, while following the cones. And as the ground swiftly approaches, with Curtis and other crew members watching, she flares the wing-cape up, which causes her legs to drop down, and then she pulls the wing-cape down to suddenly slow her glide. With the sudden decrease in speed, she—almost in like fashion to a graceful bird descending to the ground—lands on both feet while skidding to a stop. The team cheers as they tackle her with hugs. Even above the roar of their voices, Schuyler finds herself lost in her thoughts:

I'll never forget when I saw that man fall... If tragedy could lead to inspiration, how much more can a dream fulfilled help others do the impossible?

○

Powersuit Technologies. Later that evening...

Schuyler packs up her things at her desk as Curtis walks into her office and knocks on the doorway.

"Hey," he says while leaning against the wall. "What you did today... I still can't get it out of my head. There was something about your flight that seemed truly inspiring."

"Well, I couldn't have done it without you," Schuyler smiles before looking away with a bit of hesitation.

"What's wrong?" Curtis asks with wrinkled eyebrows.

"Nothing really," she replies. "It's just... I want to talk with you about something... but it's confidential."

"By now you should know you can trust me," Curtis answers

while standing up from the wall. "Do I need to sit down for this?"

"That might be a good idea."

"You're not in any trouble are you?"

"No!" Schuyler laughs almost hysterically. "This is nothing like that!"

"Whew!" Curtis exclaims as he wipes his forehead and pulls up a chair next to one of the workbenches in the office. "That makes me feel better!" he chuckles.

Schuyler reaches into her bag and pulls out a green folder. She holds it tightly to her chest. "This is a design I came up with for another flight idea." She hands it to him.

Curtis takes the folder and suddenly stops as a memory flashes through his mind. "All of this reminds me of 9th grade—the first time I came to my physics teacher, Mr. Grabowski, with my idea for the Kinetic Redistribution Boots. That changed everything for me. Now, I wonder where your design will take us?"

He opens the folder and looks at the first diagram and its description. "This is nice," he smiles. "Hey, this looks similar to the Mach-2 design."

"It is," Schuyler smiles enthusiastically. "I've been thinking about this possibility since you described how the jet-assisted thrusters on the Mach-2 work. Then I saw the videos for the Flyboard Air."

"Right," Curtis agrees. "I've seen them too. It was created by Franky Zapata. Pretty impressive."

"Yes. The Flyboard Air is awesome, but it's a platform that you strap your feet onto. You can't just land and walk around. And then there's Richard Browning of Gravity Industries. He invented the Gravity flight suit which uses four jets strapped to his arms and

94

two strapped to his lower back."

"Yes," Curtis agrees again. "I've seen his videos as well. It's great what he's been able to do. But his suit is a bit bulky. Actually, the Flyboard Air uses six jets as well. Four for thrust and two for manuevering."

"That's why I think this design will work," Schuyler replies. "You already have the foundation with the Mach-2. With these modifications, you should be able to achieve a flight time longer than 30 seconds. Although, using thrust alone to fly isn't the most efficient way to get around."

"But it will get the job done," Curtis replies. "I don't know how I didn't realize this. You know, this could work for an idea I've been mulling over for the past year and a half. What if we used this design to help first responders? Can you imagine how much good can be done if police and fire-fighters had the ability to fly?"

"Wow," Schuyler smiles, "that sounds like a great application for this design! I figured you'd use this design to modify the Mach-2."

"Hmmm, maybe. But I've been waiting to pitch this flying first-responder idea to the mayor, police commissioner and fire chief. Honestly, I couldn't figure out a design I was happy with presenting. I mainly focused on modifying existing quadcopter designs and came up with one I liked. It's a backpack with eight mini rotors that flip out when in use.

"But, we encountered some balance issues. The pack flew well by itself, but once we strapped it on a person, it kept tilting forward."

"It was too front heavy," Schuyler concludes.

"Right," Curtis agrees. "We offset the rotors, which corrected the problem, but that put too much strain on the hinges.

Ultimately, we decided, for first responders working in close proximity to people, that the flight pack had too many moving parts. I kept imagining someone's finger or other body part coming in contact with the spinning rotor blades. The project was shelved and I moved on to other things. But, I think your idea could work! It's definitely more compact than my design."

"And it shouldn't have any major balance issues!" Schuyler grins. "I'm glad you like it."

"You continue to prove that you are a valuable member of the team! Let's see what we can do with this."

Two Months Later. Mayor's Office. April 19, 2019.

Curtis and Schuyler sit on one side of a large conference table. The mayor, police comissioner and fire chief sit on the other side.

"It's good to see one of Atlanta's superstar citizens," the mayor smiles broadly. "And Ms. Watkins continues to make a name for herself. I have brought the comissioner and chief up to speed regarding our last conversation, Mr. Powers. So, please proceed."

"Thank you Mr. Mayor," Curtis replies with a strong smile. "Schuyler and I appreciate you all taking time out of your busy schedules to meet with us. As you know, we are both from New York, but Atlanta has become our home. We love it here because the city continues to be a beacon for culture, education, creativity and innovation. Atlanta is full of great people and it has always been our desire to inspire people everywhere so they can strive to reach their full potential. Having said that, allow us to introduce you to the future."

With the click of a button on Schuyler's laptop computer, the large flat screen television mounted to the conference room wall comes to life as a video begins to play:

WHAT IF FIRST RESPONDERS WERE ABLE TO HELP PEOPLE IN 3 DIMENSIONS?

A fully rendered 3D image of a police officer wearing a futuristic looking bodysuit with an integrated flight pack appears on the screen. It slowly rotates, revealing every angle of the suit.

IMAGINE POLICE OFFICERS HAVING THE ABILITY TO PATROL THE STREETS AND SKIES.

Atlanta police cars drive down several streets followed by four officers trailing them in the sky. The patrol cars stop at a building as two thieves are trying to make their getaway. The thieves run into the building and up to the roof, where they are apprehended by the four flying officers.

IMAGINE FIREFIGHTERS WITH NO HEIGHT LIMITATIONS WHEN DEALING WITH FIRES.

Another scene shows firemen attempting to put out a fire at a burning building. They are unable to reach the higher floors with their hoses. Then the flying officers arrive and provide assistance with getting the fire under control by using portable extinguishers.

IMAGINE POLICE AND COMMUNITY WORKING TOGETHER IN A NEW WAY.

Another scene shows the officers as they fly through the city— past buildings—as people wave to them and they wave back. Two flight officers land in dramatic fashion as a group of smiling kids and adults run over to greet them.

THE TOOL OF THE FUTURE IS HERE TODAY.

THE LIFT JACKET FLIGHT PACK.

IMAGINE THE POSSIBILITIES...

The video ends.

"Very nice," the mayor exclaims.

"Yes," the fire chief agrees.

"I love the concept," the police comissioner states, "but as nice as that was, it's just a computer generated video. Do you have a working prototype? And if so, how far have you come with it?"

Schuyler and Curtis smile at each other as she presses play on the next video.

"This is *actual footage* from our lab."

In the video, Schuyler stands amidst a small group of technicians, wearing a padded bodysuit and helmet. She finishes strapping on the flight pack as the team members double check all connections. With a 5-count, she engages the thrusters, which roar to life, and rises effortlessly into the air. She ascends to about thirty feet above a large foam pit stationed nearby and performs several figure eight maneuvers. Then she lands in the exact spot where she began.

The video ends as Curtis and Schuyler observe the three men sitting in front of them. Their mouths are slightly ajar and their eyes are wide open.

"So, what do you think?" Curtis inquires.

"This... looks promising," the police comissioner responds.

"What is the flight time?" the fire chief asks.

"Right now, the Lift Jacket can fly its wearer for 10 minutes between charges," Curtis responds. "We expect to reach 15-20 minutes by increasing battery capacity, without adding too much weight. But you can cover a lot of ground in 10 minutes. We are also developing a quick-charging system."

"Is it flammable?" the chief asks. "I wouldn't want anyone getting cooked during a flyby."

"The entire system is completely electric," Schuyler replies. "We created special micro-compressor centrifugal turbines which draw in huge amounts of surrounding air. That air gets pressurized and propelled through four specially designed nozzles to produce thrust. The Lift Jacket has minimal moving parts, which makes for an excellent first responder tool. You don't have to worry about bystanders getting too close to the unit."

"Is it easy to operate?" the comissioner asks as the mayor looks on with a quiet smile.

"Absolutely," Curtis answers as he looks at Schuyler. "How many hours of training did it take you?"

"Full transparency," Schuyler begins. "There were some scrapes and bruises along the way. The video you just watched showcased the 23rd iteration of the Lift Jacket design. We pretty much have worked out all of the kinks. There were some balancing issues during high wind simulations which needed some added gyroscopic stabilization.

"But it's really intuitive to use. Just like riding a bike, really. I got the hang of it after about thirty minutes. Really felt comfortable after a couple of hours. And began to master the flight dynamics after a few days."

"I tested the Lift Jacket as well," Curtis interjects. "The results were pretty much the same for me."

"Who would train my officers to fly?" the comissioner asks. "You, Mr. Powers?"

"Me?" Curtis replies with a slight chuckle. "No. Not me. Schuyler will do it. She pioneered how to use the Lift Jacket and has the most flight time in it. She was born to fly."

"So," the mayor interjects, "I am curious why you are presenting this idea to us and not the military?"

"First, I don't like the idea of my inventions being weaponized through military involvement." Curtis grows quiet before continuing. "Second, when I was a teen, there was a fire in a high-rise building. The firemen couldn't get to all of the people in time. And the ladders couldn't reach those on the highest floors. A lot of people died that day. I'd like to think if this kind of technology existed back then, most-if-not-all of the people could have been saved."

"And with everything going on these days between law enforcement and regulare everyday citizens," Schuyler adds, "we all could use some inspiration."

"And let's be honest," Curtis interjects, "for all of the great people in our city, there are those who... deliberately choose to make poor choices which affect the well being and safety of others."

"What a diplomatic way of putting that," the mayor chuckles. "Perhaps you should run for political office."

"Thank you," Curtis smiles. "But as you like to say, I know how to stay in my lane."

Everyone laughs.

"But," Curtis continues, "we all know that when people feel safe, they are free to be inspired, to inspire and to innovate."

"So," the police comissioner replies rather somberly, "what do you think the criminal element in this city will do if you give my officers the ability to fly? Do you believe they're just going to roll over and take it?"

"Hmm," Curtis responds. "Honestly, I didn't think about that."

"You didn't think about that?" the comissioner scoffs. "You're Curtis Powers! A prodigy whiz kid whose been on the cover of major magazines! You get paid to think things through and you're telling me you didn't even consider how criminals would react to your little idea?"

"Actually, I was so focused on keeping people safe and inspiring them, that I didn't stop to fully consider the issue. I don't see why we can't work through it together. But, let me ask you a question: Do the police in this city allow the criminals to dictate how they do their jobs?"

The comissioner stares at Curtis as a slight smirk forms on his lips. "Touché, Mr. Powers. So, tell us what are you proposing."

☊

11 Months Later... March 2020. City Hall. Atlanta. 10:00am.

It is a gorgeous morning as the sun shines brightly in a deep blue sky that's punctuated by occasional white puffy clouds. The Atlanta city skyline sits in the distance, with its numerous buildings and windows reflecting the sun. A large crowd—made up of reporters, business owners, and everyday citizens—is gathered in front of city hall. The mayor of Atlanta stands at a podium with

101

the police commissioner, fire chief, Curtis, Schuyler and a host of city and law enforcement officials. An empty raised platform is stationed next to them. Bright lights shine from media cameras as all present are filled with great anticipation of the mayor's surprise announcement. At the appointed time, the mayor begins his speech.

"Thank you all for attending this press conference. I know many of you are wondering what could be so important that the mayor would do this on such short notice. Well, what I have to say is for the benefit of our entire city and quite possibly our nation."

"You're running for President!" One of the reporters blurts out. The crowd's hushed response is immediate.

"No," the mayor chuckles, "I am *not* running for President of the United States. I do know how to stay in my lane."

Laughter rolls through the crowd as everyone's anticipation and curiosity is piqued.

"Now, if no one interrupts, I will quickly get to the point of this announcement. Thirteen months ago, Mr. Curtis Powers came to me with an idea. He pitched that idea and I immediately saw its potential. Two months later, he and his senior specialist project manager—Ms. Schuyler Watkins, gave the police commissioner, fire chief and myself a demonstration of his idea. We agreed to move forward to bring that vision to life. Now, please turn your attention to the top of the skyscraper approximately eight hundred yards from here."

The mayor smiles broadly, while pointing to the building in the distance as everyone turns around. "Ladies and gentlemen, may I present to you, two of our city's finest!"

The crowd is confused, not knowing what to expect, as

102

movement can be seen on the roof. Two objects rise from the top of the building and begin to make their way, through the air, to the crowd.

"What are those?" several people shout. "Are they drones?" Cameramen gasp as the objects come into view through their telephoto lenses.

"Those aren't objects!" a reporter yells. "Those are people!"

Within moments, two police officers are clearly visible as they streak through the air and fly over the hushed, wide-eyed crowd. The hum of their flight pack engines are heard as they crisscross their flight trajectory, circle around the crowd in dramatic fashion and then hover above the awaiting platform. In the midst of their flight packs' jet wash they land with the ease and agility of a helicopter. The engines disengage and grow quiet amidst the crowd's staggering applause.

The two officers—one male and the other female—stand before the people, wearing futuristic looking blue and black police uniforms with flashing LED lights built into their shoulder pads.

"For the last ten months," the mayor declares, "we have worked with Powersuit Technologies to develop the world's first-ever First Responders Aerial Unit. Imagine police officers being able to fly! Flight will open up many opportunities and benefits for community patrol, fire safety and disaster relief response! Criminals beware. Good citizens can rest a little bit easier because the 3rd Division Aerial Unit is here!

"Beginning in September, 3rd Division will be a year-long pilot program, here in our great city. It will consist of twenty-four Flight Officers—each partnered together—who will patrol the streets from the air and assist our fire fighters when needed. A program support team will ensure they are utilized across the city in the most efficient way possible. The program will be monitored and assessed over the year. Once it is complete, we will determine if it has helped to make our communities safer. If it has, then the program will continue on a year-by-year basis and will roll out to other cities large enough to warrant having flying first responders."

Eager reporters blurt out a multiplicity of questions.

"How do the flight packs work?"

"What criteria will you use to pick suitable officers?"

"How long can a person stay in the air?"

"Where is the funding coming from for this pilot program?"

"Ladies and gentlemen of the press," the mayor interjects with a strong smile while raising his hands in a calming fashion, "all of your questions will be answered when this program officially launches in September. The purpose of this press conference today is to provide you with a basic understanding of what is to come. The next generation of law enforcement and fire fighting is here. And it is the 3rd Division Aerial Unit!"

The two Officers activate their Lift Jackets and rise effortlessly into the sky as the jet wash from their flight packs rushes over the cheering crowd. The officers salute with a smile and streak back to the skyscraper. Once they are out of sight, the mayor, police commissioner, fire chief, Curtis, Schuyler and other officials take photos as the press conference ends.

Later that day. Powersuit Technologies. 2:30pm.

"Alright people," Curtis smiles as he addresses his employees in the company auditorium, "I know we have a number of projects that we are working on. As you already know, we will be going through some restructuring in order to make sure there's enough bandwidth to handle our current projects and provide technical support to the 3rd Division Aerial Pilot Program. All of you have done an excellent job so far! Please... please... please... please keep up the good work."

Everyone laughs.

"It's Friday! Go home early and enjoy your weekend!"

As everyone exits the auditorium, Curtis approaches Schuyler.

"Hey. Two things. First, I have something for you to see on Monday."

"Cool. What is it?"

"Not telling."

"Okay... I like suprises. What's the second thing?"

"I have to go to New York June 28th to July 2nd to check on a project I'm consulting on. You want to come?"

"Sure," Schuyler smiles. "What's the project?"

"Sorry. That's classified. I can't tell you until we get there. But there's a lot we still have to do with 3rd Division, before we leave for the Big Apple."

"This is finally happening," Schuyler utters with a nervous smile.

"Yes it is," Curtis agrees. "A combination of both of our dreams. Don't tell me you're getting cold feet."

"No," Schuyler replies. "I just think the enormity of it all is starting to hit me. I hope I can live up to your expectations."

"I hope I can live up to my own," Curtis chuckles. "You have done well so far. You will do well going forward. Can I give you some advice?"

"Please," she laughs. "I'll take all I can get!"

They begin walking from the auditorium to their offices.

"As you know, one of the things my wife does is teach dance. Kelly's been a dancer since she was a little girl and she loves it. But, when we were in high school, there came a time when she didn't love it anymore. The pressure to perform had grown so heavy. Everyone had expectations for her to be great and she became afraid to fail. Dancing had turned into a chore to her.

"When she told me about all of the pressure she was under, I asked her what it was about dance that drew her to it in the first place? She shared a wonderful story about how, as a little girl it made her feel like a princess. That's when I told her, what I'm about to tell you: **Whatever you do, do it because you love it otherwise you will grow to hate it.** Schuyler, you *love* flight! *Never* lose sight of that, even when other people have their expectations of you and what they think you should be doing. And if you find something to love in all of your endeavors, you will be successful, no matter the outcome."

Both of them grab their bags and walk out of the building towards the parking lot. Their cars sit side by side.

"Thank you for taking a chance on me," Schuyler says while extending her hand.

Curtis smiles as he shakes her hand. "A boatload of people took a chance on me. And they still do—everyday. I'm just trying to pay it forward. As my father would always tell me, 'Do your best so the miraculous can happen.'"

"What did your father mean by that statement?"

Curtis leans back on his car. "He meant that if we work with a spirit of excellence, then God will open doors for us."

"You really believe that?"

"I do. The Bible confirms it over and over again."

"Well, it's great you have that kind of assurance and confidence." She chuckles with a shake of her head. "Is it possible that your dad's statement works for some and not for others?"

"I think having a spirit of excellence works for everybody. God doesn't play favorites. He loves everyone the same. And he gives each of us gifts and talents to exploit in order to make an impact *and* a living. However, our decisions about coming to him determine how much of his reality and provision we experience."

Curtis' watch buzzes as a text comes through. He glances at it. "Sorry. That's Kelly. I've got to go. We can talk more about this later if you like."

Schuyler nods her head slightly with a smile as she waves goodbye. Curtis opens his car door and waves back.

"Hey, Curtis!"

He stops halfway inside his car and stands back up. "Yeah?"

Schuyler stares at him for a moment. "At some point, I think I'd like to hear more about this relationship with Jesus thing."

"Whenever you're ready," he smiles. "Have a great weekend!"

Curtis gets in his car and starts the engine. Schuyler enters her vehicle and does the same. She watches as he drives away while honking his horn twice. She honks back with a wave and puts her car in gear. As she begins to pull away from her parking spot she whispers to herself: "Could it really be that simple?"

Chapter Eight

TOUCHING THE SKY

"I'm not playing with death, I'm playing with life." - Yves Rossy (Jetman)

Monday morning. Curtis' Workshop.

"So, what's the big surprise?" Schuyler asks as she enters the work station.

Curtis points near his worktable. A tall, shrouded figure rests next to it. Schuyler smiles while walking over and removing the sheet. A mannequin stands before her, wearing her flight harness and wing-cape.

"It's my flight harness."

"Turn it around," Curtis smiles with a motion of his hand.

Schuyler does so, pulling the cape aside—revealing several modifications. "Are those compressor jets?"

"I miniaturized the ones from the Lift Jacket by 25% and connected them to four nozzles which are attached to the hip straps. They don't have as much thrust, but they should give you a good burst of speed and offset at least two-thirds of your weight."

"And that," she exclaims as the pieces come together in her mind, "will extend my flight time!" Schuyler pulls out her tablet and goes to Youtube. "Have you seen these?"

Curtis walks over from his desk and watches several videos of men jumping out of airplanes and flying in wing suits—landing without a parachute. One of them lands on water. The other lands on a large strip of 18,000 cardboard boxes.

Curtis gulps. "You want to do *that*?"

"*You* made the upgrades," Schuyler laughs.

"Yeah," Curtis agrees, "so you could fly down the side of a larger mountain for a longer period of time."

"If these new jets work, I can finally soar through the air like a bird... and hopefully land safely."

"I don't know," Curtis mumbles as he points at the tablet's screen. "*That* is dangerous."

"It's a calculated risk," Schuyler confidently replies. "Just like everything else we do. And just like *your* Powersuits. But..." she says with a rise in her voice, "if you help me, I know I can do this."

Curtis stares at her silently.

"I don't know..."

Schuyler shakes her head. "When a guy like Jetman teaches himself to fly through the air with a homemade wing strapped to his back, you say *that's* cool. But when I want to do the same thing with my own design, you say it's too dangerous? It's because I'm a woman. You think I can't handle it?"

"It's not that," Curtis replies.

Schuyler crosses her arms and cocks her head at an angle, "Then what is it?"

Curtis huffs. "I didn't know Yves Rossy when he did what he

did. But I *do* know you. If something happens to you... I don't know what I'd do. Then I'd have to be the one to tell your father."

"Don't bring my dad into this," Schuyler interjects. "I'm an adult. You said yourself that I was born to fly. If you really believe that, then help me do this."

Curtis sits back at his desk and stares into Schuyler's eyes.

"Come on, Curtis," she pleads. "I have over twenty hours experience flying in a vertical wind tunnel. I've flown a hang glider and I've glided down the side of large hills and a mountain in my wing-cape. I can do this! But I need your help to pull it off."

Curtis shakes his head slightly while biting his lip. "I can't believe I'm going to say it."

Schuyler smiles with wide eyes. "Yes?"

"If I help you, we have to approach this with the utmost caution. This isn't like gliding down the side of a hill. And your wing-cape may not be as efficient as a full-sized hang glider. If you make *one* error—just one, or the wing-cape malfunctions at that height, and you don't have a parachute, you could die."

"So, is that a yes?"

Curtis breathes heavily while slowly nodding his head. "Yes."

Schuyler jumps with a shout of jubilation. "YES!"

"We're going to need help," Curtis adds as he picks up his cell phone. "The R & D department is already working at full capacity."

"So, how are we going to do this without the manpower?"

"I'll have to call in another team."

111

Ten days later... Late at night. After work hours.

Schuyler yawns as she enters Curtis' private workshop.

"You wanted to see me?"

"Wow," he utters from his desk. "You look tired."

"It's been a long week," she yawns again. "I am so glad the weekend is almost here. Do you see the bags under my eyes?"

"I can see them," Curtis smiles sympathetically. "But tonight is the perfect time to get started on your project."

"I thought we were starting tomorrow when everyone arrived."

Curtis motions for her to turn around. In an instant, she is wide-eyed, fully awake, and beyond excited!

"They came a day early," Curtis laughs.

"I feel like I'm gonna explode!" Schuyler smacks her face in astonishment at the sight. Her dream team steps out of the shadows and stands in front of her, at the ready.

"It's nice to finally meet you," Omar Powers smiles as he shakes her hand. His presence towers over her. "I'm Curtis' older brother."

"Welcome to the family," Miranda cheers as she and Kelly give Schuyler hugs.

"We've heard so much about you," Kelly adds.

In rapid succession, everyone introduces themselves.

"This," Curtis replies with a broad smile, "is Team Speedsuit!"

112

"So," Mr. Grabowski inquires, "what's this new project Curtis has been so secretive about?"

"Are we working on 3rd Division?" Gavin asks.

"No," Curtis replies, "we have a team to handle that."

"So, what is it?" Treyshawn asks.

Curtis motions to a corner of the workshop as Schuyler pulls a sheet off of the mannequin, revealing her modified flight harness and wing-cape.

"I need you to help prepare for a world record attempt. Schuyler is going to jump out of a helicopter at 12,000 feet, fly through the air and land without a parachute."

"Are you serious?" Treyshawn balks.

"Crazy, I know," Curtis chuckles, "but the numbers check out."

"It's doable," Schuyler agrees, "however, we can't do this alone."

"What's the timeframe?" Kelly asks.

"Use the entire month of May to prepare: secure the location, get the permits, a ton of wind tunnel testing, contact the world record people, etc... Then do the actual flight the first weekend in June—weather permitting."

"You know," Treyshawn declares, "this would sound crazy to normal people."

"Nothing we've done in the last 11 years has been normal," Omar replies.

"Ain't that the truth," Miranda utters as everyone else agrees. "Well," she continues, "we flew all this way. We might as well get to work."

Saturday, June 6th. Two hours until the world record attempt.

A crowd of spectators begin to gather in a field next to a large hangar. Inside, a team of volunteers tasked with successfully pulling off this event receive their final instructions. All preparations have been set as the meeting ends with a prayer. The group of over fifty people stand silently. Many bow their heads. Others rest their arms behind their backs out of respect.

"God," Curtis begins, "thank you for the opportunity to do something amazing today! Thank you for everyone who has come to help make this dream a reality. Please keep all of us safe from dangers seen and unseen. *Especially* keep Schuyler safe. May her actions today help inspire an entire generation toward greatness! In Jesus' name we pray. Amen."

The group responds with a collective "Amen" and a cheer as they break into their separate ranks and begin to take their assigned positions. Schuyler prepares to suit up as a car arrives outside. Curtis runs to meet the vehicle's occupants and then returns with them.

"Hey Schuyler," he announces, "there's some people here who want to see you."

She turns around to find her dad, brother and mother standing in front of her with all smiles.

"Dad? Mom? Tyler?" She exclaims. "What are you doing here?"

"What are *we* doing here?" her dad counters, "what are *you* doing here?"

"Yeah," her mom adds, "how come you didn't call to tell us about all of this?"

"Yeah, Sis," Tyler interjects with a smirk, "that was real shady."

"I didn't call because I didn't want you to worry! I was going to tell you guys after we set the world record!"

"Well, Curtis called us and told us *everything*," Schuyler's mom says with a bit of fake attitude.

"When we set our world record back in high school," Curtis interjects, "my mom was there to see it. I felt it was only right to bring your family down."

"And," Schuyler's dad states, "he gave us strict orders NOT to worry you!"

They all laugh.

"Well," Schuyler responds as she grabs them up in a big group hug, "in that case, I'm really glad you guys are here!"

After a bit more smalltalk, Curtis escorts Schuyler's family out to the viewing area, while she focuses on suiting up and testing all of her flight systems. Just over an hour later, she is ready to go.

Flight Time...

The deep blue sky stretches as far as the eye can see... puffy white clouds pepper the expanse like wafts of cotton candy at a carnival.

Schuyler stands—tethered to the side of a helicopter—as it ascends into the sky. The warm sunlight bathes her smiling face and reflects off of her new multi-colored flight suit. Miniature cameras sit on both sides of her helmet, recording everything she sees. The rapidly spinning helicopter rotors whip the wind around her as her wing-cape billows back and forth. Curtis' voice rings over her earpiece while she scans the surrounding countryside below.

"Are you okay?" Curtis' sits inside the aircraft, several feet away from her perch. Large headphones cover his ears.

"Never felt better," Schuyler responds. "Everything looks so different from 12,000 feet up in the air."

Curtis nods his head in agreement. "Very different from standing on top of a hill."

"That's an understatement," she chuckles with a slight hint of nervousness rolling in her voice.

Down on the ground, a full six miles from Schuyler's helicopter, a sizable crowd awaits: spectators, media reporters, Powersuit Technologies employees, first responders, and world record personnel eagerly anticipate Schuyler's descent. Large screens are stationed throughout the crowd, which display the video feed from two other helicopters near Schuyler and Curtis' aircraft. To the side of the group sits a long strip of cardboard boxes and foam that's twenty feet thick and almost the size of a football field. This is where Schuyler will land... without a parachute.

Back in the sky, Schuyler closes the visor on her helmet as Curtis' voice sounds over her communications array.

"You should be able to glide for over six miles before needing to land. That's double the distance an average wing suit can traverse from this height. That's also *without* using your compressor jets. Once you activate them, that should extend your time, distance and maneuverability even more. Are you ready?"

"Yep," Schuyler shouts. "Is everything else ready to go?"

Curtis calls to each team member. Everyone responds in the affirmative. Cameras are rolling. Vitals are being tracked. First responders are on standby.

"We're ready," Curtis confirms as he grabs his binoculars.

"Here we go," Schuyler exclaims as she unhooks the tether, leaps from the helicopter and drops into an overwhelming feeling of weightlessness. Her wing-cape fills with air within seconds as her body arcs and takes horizontal flight. She stretches her arms out to her sides like wings as she glides the deep blue sky like a surfer rides a wave. The sound of her body rushing through the atmosphere drowns out her laughter as she banks into a left turn and then turns to the right. Her altitude, speed and battery levels display on her helmet's visor.

The three helicopters trail her from different angles as Curtis' voice comes over her earpiece again. "Schuyler! How is it? Are you okay?"

"I'm great!" she laughs. "This is amazing! Absolutely amazing!"

On the ground, the crowd looks at the large display screens. Tyler can't help but get lost in the moment as he sees his sister hurtling through the sky.

"Wow, Sis," he whispers with a smile. "You're doing it… What you dreamed about for years… you're doing it."

Curtis watches Schuyler through his binoculars and on a screen in the helicopter cabin.

"You've been descending this entire time," he announces. "It's time to use the jets."

"Copy that!" Schuyler answers. "Powering up the jets in 5, 4, 3, 2, 1!" With the press of a button she activates the dual compressors on her harness. They rev up as the thrust immediately kicks through the nozzles on her hips. Schuyler's body accelerates forward as she arches her back and begins to climb through the air. She shoots her arms forward in classic superhero fashion as she changes the angle of attack on her wing-cape and carries out a full loop before swooping toward a nearby stack of clouds.

"I'm flying!" She laughs as she streaks through the white puffiness. "I'm really flying!" As she pierces through the other side of the clouds, she banks right and veers toward her designated target—a full three miles away. Suddenly, out of the corner of her eye, she sees a flock of geese flying above her. A moment later, she joins their formation and soars six to ten feet from them: so close she can hear the distinct flapping of their wings and the honk of their calls.

"Schuyler!" Curtis shouts from his helicopter. "You are *flying* with geese!"

"I know," she laughs. "Isn't it great? I'm flying with geese! This is a dream come true!"

"This video is going to be epic," Curtis replies.

"I know, right!" Schuyler agrees.

"But it's time to get ready to land. You're almost a full two miles out from the landing strip."

"Copy that," Schuyler answers. "Well geese, it was great flying with you!" At that point a thought crosses her mind, causing her to smile broadly. With a shift of her weight, she glides closer to the goose nearest to her and reaches out her hand.

Curtis watches with a curious discomfort. "What are you doing?"

"I just want to touch it," Schuyler smiles as she stretches her arm out more to reach the tail feathers of the flapping bird.

"I don't think that's a good idea..."

As the words leave his lips, Schuyler's fingers touch the goose's tail feathers. In an instant the bird startles, flaps erratically and crashes right into her helmet! She screams as the blunt impact causes her to lurch in the opposite direction as the resulting air turbulence flips her on her back. Her wing-cape wraps around her like a noose, as its tangled fabric depressurizes... She plummets out of the sky like a rock.

The crowd on the ground screams in a panic!

"No!" Curtis yells from the helicopter as he watches in horror and motions to the pilot. "Get me to her!" He looks at the altimeter as the helicopter dives in pursuit. Schuyler's screams fill Curtis' ear piece.

"Curtis!!!"

"Schuyler!" He yells back.

"I can't see!" Her body goes into an uncontrolled spin as the g-forces rapidly increase.

The helicopter reaches her altitude and now descends at the same rate of her fall. Curtis barks out commands.

"Schuyler! Listen to me!"

"I can't see!" Her voice rolls with terror. "Spinning out

of control!!"

"I know!" He yells. "I see you! Listen! At this height, we've got 60 seconds before your fall becomes unrecoverable!"

"I'm afraid!" She screams as she struggles to free herself from the smothering wing-cape.

"I know! But if you don't listen, you'll die! You've got to trust me!"

"O-Okay!!!"

"Flip on your stomach!"

"I can't see where I am!"

"You don't need to see! Remember your wind tunnel training. *Feel* your body position in space! Flip over now!"

"I'm so dizzy…"

Curtis glances at his watch. "45 seconds! You were born to fly, Schuyler! You can do this!"

"I don't know if I can…" Schuyler mumbles.

"You have to!"

"So… dizzy…"

"You've got to stay awake! 30 seconds! Flip now!"

Schuyler tries to flip, but the buffeting air overpowers her.

"20 seconds! Flip now or you're going to die!"

With all of her might, Schuyler flips onto her stomach with her arms outstretched. The crowd below and in the air cheer at the top of their lungs as her wing-cape unravels, re-pressurizes, slows her descent and generates forward momentum—helping her gain some altitude.

"Yes!" Curtis shouts. "Schuyler you did it! Now you need to bank right so you can make the landing zone."

Schuyler continues to glide on her present course. Amidst the cheering crowd on the ground, Omar and Mr. Grabowski notice a red flag on her vitals display. Back in the helicopter, Curtis continues to give directions.

"Okay Schuyler, you need to make the right turn *now*."

"Curtis!" Omar's voice sounds in his earpiece. "We think Schuyler's unconscious!"

"Schuyler?" Curtis calls as he stares intently at her body. Her arms and legs seem limp.

"Schuyler!" he yells. "Do you hear me? You need to turn right!"

Still no response.

For a second, fear overtakes Curtis. "Please Lord," he whispers, "don't let it end like this." He yells at the top of his lungs. "Schuyler, wake up!!!"

The sound of his voice rings in her ear, rousing her mind. Her eyes flutter as she regains consciousness and looks around trying to get her bearings. "Where am I?"

"You're awake!" Curtis exclaims. "You need to bank right or you'll miss the landing zone!"

Schuyler banks hard to the right as her focus sharpens on the task at hand. "Did I pass out?"

"Yes," Curtis replies. "We'll talk about that later. You need to land. And you're coming in hot!"

She sees the landing strip and the large crowd in the distance—about half a mile out.

Schuyler makes quick adjustments to line up with the landing strip. The helicopters follow nearby as her altitude steadily decreases along with her speed: 80 mph... 70 mph... 60 mph... 50 mph... She glides straight on target as the cheers from the crowd are clearly heard in the distance.

"You're still coming in too fast!" Curtis calls.

Schuyler flares out her cape at thirty-five feet above the ground, as she slows even more and begins to glide over the cardboard boxes and foam. She kicks her legs down and activates her jets which rotate forward for greater deceleration. Still, she clears most of the landing strip, missing the targeted "X" in the center.

"I don't know if I'm gonna stop in time!" She shouts while trying to catch her feet on the boxes and foam in order to slow herself. But, her feet skip across the surface. She throttles her jets to maximum which finally slows her to under 10 miles per hour. With a last desperate attempt, she cuts her engines, retracts the wing-cape and lands on the boxes with a thud and a role, finally skidding to a stop—six feet away from the edge!

Her body heaves as she breathes heavily and stumbles to her feet. The crowd erupts into applause as she sinks into the cardboard and foam with a jubilant wave.

The surrounding helicopters land as the team works to extricate Schuyler from the boxes. Moments later, she walks free while removing her helmet, as her family almost runs her over to give her a flurry of hugs. Curtis and Team Speedsuit join them in a massive group embrace. As tears fill all of their eyes, media personnel swarm around them for a paparazzi-styled photo-op.

The World Record representatives approach to confirm her flight.

"Schuyler Watkins! You are the first person in a wing-cape to fly from an aircraft, over six miles and land safely without a parachute! Congratulations on setting this world record! And we are glad your attempt did not end in disaster!"

The crowd celebrates her monumental achievement as a number of local reporters interview her before she heads back to the hangar in the distance. All the while, she is lost in her thoughts:

Some people thought I'd never make it here. They said my head was too far up in the clouds. They laughed. They scorned. Yet, here I am literally soaring through the clouds! Some of those same people could never rise above the drama in their own lives. Now they are stuck with broken dreams while I'm here living my own. Somehow, I believed this was possible… and with determination, support from those who believe in me, and hard work… here I am.

Where will things go from here? I don't know. But there is one thing I am sure of: I want to teach others how to fly! Not just with this invention, but more importantly with their lives! And not just those who already believed in me… but those who stood in opposition to me as well.

By 6pm her face is plastered all over the news. By the 11 o'clock news, her video has been viewed online over 500,000 times. By morning, her flight had been viewed over 3 million times. By Monday, a number of television producers call Powersuit Technologies seeking to have Schuyler appear on national talk shows to discuss the significance of her flight. Who would have thought that a black girl from Brooklyn would be able to soar through the air just like a bird…And now, she had infallible proof for every naysayer who said and would *ever* say that her dream was impossible.

●

Two weeks later... Powersuit Technologies.

An exhausted Schuyler sits in her office as Curtis walks up and stops by her doorway.

"Glad to see you made it back," he smiles. "You looked great on television."

"Thank you," Schuyler forces a tired smile. "It's been a busy couple of weeks. All the talk shows and speaking engagements…"

"My favorite part was when you said 'the moral of the story was not to tug on a goose's tail feathers while it was flying.'"

Schuyler laughs. "And the host said, 'that's right up there with never bother a dog when it's eating!'"

"That was hilarious!" Curtis agrees. "But you really stood your ground in that other interview. I was proud of you."

"Thanks! Did you see the entire thing?"

●

One week earlier... Good Morning World Talk Show.

Studio lights shine brightly as a well dressed, well groomed, smiling white man with perfect hair and teeth smiles at the camera. He is sitting in a regal looking chair. Schuyler sits next to him on a plush couch. An epic image of Schuyler soaring through the air is

124

projected behind them on a wall-sized display screen.

"Good morning World! I'm Carl Rogers and I'm here with the one and only Schuyler Watkins, who set an amazing world record amidst fascinating and harrowing circumstances. Schuyler, it's good to have you here."

"Thank you!" she smiles. "It's great to be here with you today."

"Let's jump right in. You almost died when you made your world record attempt."

"That's a pretty accurate assessment," she chuckles as the image behind them changes to footage of the actual flight.

"Well, we're glad you are alive and well," the host smiles. "It's amazing what you've been able to invent and accomplish given your background."

Schuyler pauses with a forced smile. "What exactly do you mean?"

"I mean," the host replies with a nervous roll in his voice, "that you had to… overcome many obstacles to get to this place."

"I'll admit," she replies in a slightly relaxed tone, "the obstacles do make for a better story. But shouldn't my accomplishments be amazing just because I've done something no one else has done before? Or by 'background' are you saying that the expectation is extremely low—even non-existent for someone from an urban environment who is also a black woman?"

The host forces an uncomfortable grin as he looks at the camera and then back at her. "That… is not what I meant."

"Perhaps," Schuyler smiles politely, "but that seems to be what you implied."

"Okay," the host breathes deeply while regaining his composure, "let's talk about that for a moment. What you have done is unprecedented. The worlds of skydiving, hang gliding and wing suit flying are mainly populated by white men and some women, but very few persons of color."

"Sure," Schuyler agrees. "I don't think it's intentional, it is just what it is. But the general expectation when it comes to aeronautical innovation is that it is primarily a world that is dominated by men. Women are there, but in much smaller amounts. And black women—even less.

"Some people look at what I've done and say, 'there's no way a black girl from Brooklyn did this.' They think that I stole my wing-cape design from some white guy. But what I've done is the result of years of study and observation. It's also the result of years of inspiration provided by my father who—once he saw how much I loved flight—did everything within his power to expose me to every aspect of aerodynamics. He also used books to introduce me to great pioneers of aviation: from Bessie Coleman, to Amelia Earhart, to the Wright Brothers and beyond."

"Well said," the host interjects.

"Thank you," Schuyler smiles, "but I'm not finished. Just two more things I would like to say."

"Go right ahead," the host chuckles at her straight-forwardness, "We have just over a minute left."

"Some people believe invention and innovation belong to white people or the privileged economic elite. This is one of the reasons why there's an imbalance of resource and opportunity acquisition in our educational system. But, as a black woman, I am part of an ethnic group who—historically—has been inventing and innovating in every sector of civilization in every country where we live. We could take up your entire show just listing all the people of color who have made such lasting contributions.

"Second… Invention and innovation are what happens when you marry imagination and observation with execution. They are not restricted by color, gender or even economics. Anyone can do them. This is why they are so amazing. At whatever level you are in life, wherever you're from, whatever obstacles you have had to overcome… you can use your mind to invent and innovate. What I've been able to do proves this to be true."

"We are out of time. Thank you for sharing your insights with us! Congratulations again on your monumental achievement. Ladies and gentlemen—Schuyler Watkins!"

The present. Powersuit Technologies.

"I guess I did handle that situation pretty well."

"You sure did," Curtis agrees. "You were confident and knowledgeable."

"I was also terrified!"

"Really?" Curtis balks. "You didn't look it."

"Yes, well, I'm just glad it's over." Schuyler breathes a sigh of relief. "The last two weeks were amazing and exhausting! I do look forward to getting some much needed sleep."

"All the things we don't think about when we set a major world record," Curtis chuckles. "Same thing happened to me after I did the exhibition run at the 2012 Olympics."

"How did you deal with the media frenzy back then?"

"One day at a time," Curtis laughs. "Seriously... one day at a time. Don't forget we go to New York next week. Go ahead and take tomorrow to catch up on rest. I need you sharp."

"I think I'll take you up on that," Schuyler chuckles. "And again... thank you for saving my life."

"You've thanked me already."

"And I will *keep* thanking you as long as I live. If it wasn't for you..." she looks away as tears swell in her eyes. "Things would have been very different."

Curtis fights back his own tears. "Well, you're welcome... again!"

They stare at each other for a few moments—reliving the adventure in their minds.

"That was crazy," Curtis whispers.

"It was," Schuyler agrees.

"But... it was absolutely awesome too!" he exclaims. "Just... wait to pet the geese when they're on the ground from now on."

"Oh, you don't have to tell me twice!" Schuyler laughs as she wipes her eyes and takes a deep breath. "So, how's 3rd Division been going while I was away?"

"Everything's pretty much on schedule. We just moved into the new command center. And we started testing the new drone prototypes. So far, they're working like we envisioned. Officer applications are being accepted and reviewed. Flight training will begin July 6th."

"That's awesome," Schuyler responds. "I'm glad things are going as planned. I'll head to the lab and take a look at everything."

"You do that," Curtis smiles. "So, now that you've reached this pinnacle, what's next on your list of flight dreams?"

"I dunno," Schuyler shrugs. "I'd love to go to Kill Devil Hills near Kitty Hawk, North Carolina. It's the birthplace of modern aviation where Wilber and Orville Wright had their first flight. But right now, I'm just riding this wave for a bit. After the wave stops, I would like to *perfect* the dream."

"You looked pretty perfect flying with those geese. I've been meaning to ask you... What was it like?"

Schuyler takes a deep breath as she recollects her thoughts. "How do I describe it? Soaring through the air with the wind at my fingertips, surrounded by miles and miles of sky and clouds with the ground thousands of feet beneath me... It was freedom. Like an invitation that said: *anything is possible if you truly believe it can be done.*"

"That," Curtis smiles, "is *exactly* how I feel everytime I run down a highway at over 80 miles per hour. I hear the sound of the wind and think: *I'm wearing a suit that enables me to do what someone else considers impossible.* I mean, God has given us this beautiful world and its scientific laws to explore. And we've been given a mind to figure things out. In many ways, the only real limits we have are the ones we impose on ourselves by our small thinking."

"Like your dad said, 'Do your best so the miraculous can happen.'"

Curtis stares at Schuyler and smiles. "Yep... that's what he said. So... what do you mean about *perfecting* your dream? You want to make the wing-cape more efficient than it already is?"

"It's not so much about that," Schuyler admits. "I mean, the more efficient we can get it, the better. But, I have another idea for flight that I've been developing."

"Really?" Curtis' eyes open wide in suprise. "Something better than the wing-cape and Lift Jacket?"

"As great as they both are, they still have their limitations. I can't take off from the ground with the wing-cape. And even though the Lift Jacket *can*, it still has a maneuverability issue. If the Flight Officer's turn radius is too tight, they could have a mid-air spinout and crash."

"Right. That's why we determined the maximum safe turning angle and installed gyroscopes and sensors in the jacket to help provide stabilization. It's the best we can do with the design. But even with the limitation, the Lift Jackets are pretty amazing."

"Definitely!" Schuyler agrees with a nod of her head and a broad smile. "But I think they're just the beginning."

Curtis is at a loss for words. "So, what new idea are you proposing?"

"It's top secret," Schuyler smirks. "*Maybe* I'll tell you about it after we get back from New York."

"Seriously?" Curtis laughs.

"Just taking notes from my boss," Schuyler chuckles. "And for the record, I'm not proposing anything... yet. But I got this idea from flying in the vertical wind tunnel. If it works, it will give a person complete maneuverability in the air."

"Wow." Curtis is stunned. "You're like me with all of my Powersuits... but with flight."

"Thank you!" Schuyler laughs. "That's the best compliment ever! You know you're a straight up Blerd when it comes to

130

creating Powersuits!"

"Blerd?" Curtis responds with wrinkled eyebrows.

"A *black nerd*. It's a term of endearment, pride and strength. You're like a black Tony Stark!"

Curtis laughs heartily. "Well, you learn something new every day. Thank you! On a slightly different topic, after reviewing your world-record flight, you probably could have landed without the cardboard boxes."

"I thought so, but I wasn't completely sure. Better safe than sorry. You know, we should make another wing-cape so you can try it out."

"Wha—?" Curtis almost chokes. "Me jumping out of a helicopter at 12,000 feet? No thank you. As cool as it is... I'll stay on the ground in my Mach-2 Speedsuit."

◑

Several days later...

It's Sunday night. Curtis and Schuyler have just boarded a passenger plane and have found their seats—in first class.

"This is *nice*," Schuyler smiles as she nestles into the plush chair. "This is my first time in first class."

"It *is* nice," Curtis smiles as the flight attendant brings them rolled up hot towels on a tray and asks if they would like a beverage and a snack.

"The plane hasn't even taken off yet and they're asking us about drinks and food?"

"It's *very* different from sitting in the economy class section. And it's easier to get work done here with all the extra room."

"Wait," Schuyler's eyebrows wrinkle, "I'm surprised you don't have your own private jet."

"Private jets are expensive. We've had to rent a few in the past when necessary. For example, if I need to travel with one or more of my powersuits. But, I'm not at a level where I need a private plane all the time. Usually, I fly business class and every now and then first class."

"So," Schuyler switches subjects, "how am I supposed to be prepared for these meetings in New York if I don't know what they are about?"

Curtis looks around as he lowers his voice to a whisper. "I've been working with a tech company on a revolutionary learning device. We are going to see the final prototype in action and to discuss the next phase of production. I can't say anymore than that. I want you to observe during the meetings. Take notes. Think through possibilities and worst-case scenarios. Come to this with a clean slate—with no major expectations—that's why I haven't given you any information. You are 'fresh eyes' in a setting where everyone else has been working on this for the last couple of years. I'm hoping that gives us the ability to see what we might otherwise miss."

"Wow... thank you for the opportunity," Schuyler looks down at the floor for a moment before looking back up again. "I won't let you down."

"It's not even about that," Curtis smiles. "There's no pressure. Just be you. That's all."

The last passenger boards the plane, as the doors are secured. The plane taxis to the runway and takes off for New York.

⋒

A short while later, at an undisclosed location somewhere in the underbelly of Atlanta, Georgia.

Leaders from various criminal enterprises dispersed throughout the city gather under a tenuous agreement. It would seem that a common threat has brought them together. All are on edge, as the one who arranged the meeting enters the room, takes the obvious seat of authority and scans the group before speaking.

"We've always stayed within our own territories. We've had an *understanding...* even if that understanding has been enforced by violence. You being here tonight doesn't mean the rules have changed. I don't like most of you. You don't like me. But our common enemy is about to do something unorthodox. I called you here so we can discuss how best to respond to the mayor's grand announcement."

"Using jetpacks to help firefighters is one thing," someone utters. "I'd love to try one on. But flying cops is bad for business!"

"It's hard enough tryin' to avoid police on the streets," another interjects. "Now we gotta deal wit' em in the air?"

Everyone agrees.

"So, snuff 'em out before they get started," another suggests.

"No..." the hosting criminal counters. "Too heavy a hand too soon will yield more problems than solutions."

"Why should we listen to you?" someone calls out. "We can handle this on our own!"

"And yet, you are here..." the hosting criminal observes with a sly smile. "None of you have to listen to me. My first thought was to devise my own plans and let the police take care of whoever they catch. I even considered leaking your whereabouts to the authorities. With some of you out of the way, my work would be much easier. But, a pilot program of this magnitude which, if successful, would spread throughout the country and potentially to other countries, proves detrimental to *all* of my operations. The 3rd Division Aerial Unit must fail. And for that to happen, we need to find a way to work together."

"And what about that Powers guy?" someone questions.

"Based on previous events, it's clear to me that it is unwise and dangerous to underestimate Curtis Powers. We must assume the same thing for anyone working with him."

"Like that flight girl who set the world record," a third person mentions. "What's her name?"

"Schuyler Watkins. Absolutely. Right now, she and Mr. Powers are on a plane to New York for a series of meetings."

"So, what do we do?" another huffs. "I just got outta prison and business is good. I ain't tryin' to go back."

Silence lingers as the one who called the meeting broods over his thoughts before answering.

"Let them fly! We'll use this situation to our advantage. From my experience, a 'crash and burn' is always a more spectacular spectacle. You see, that's the problem with flight: what goes up must always come back down."

FROM AUTHOR TO READER...

Thank you for reading the next installment in this epic urban adventure story! My Speedsuit Powers story initially started as one book, and then grew into three. Before and during the writing of the trilogy I had a host of other stories and characters perculating in my mind. When I started working on Book 3, a friend suggested bringing my other characters into an expanded world.

One Speedsuit Powers super-fan declared that the trilogy coming to an end was bitter-sweet. She was excited to see how the story concludes, but she was sad that the trilogy would be over. Though this trilogy has come to an end, the world of Speedsuit Powers is just opening up! New characters and storylines are now being introduced. These stories are separate, but take place in the same world as Curtis, Treyshawn and the rest of the Speedsuit Team. There may be some crossovers... At the very least, there will be some reference to the trilogy. After all, Curtis' future is just getting started. So stay tuned! The next few years look quite promising. The Speedsuit Powers Expanded Universe has begun!

Sincerely,

Allen Paul Weaver III

Author, Speedsuit Powers Trilogy & Flight

Reader's Guide
Selected Themes

Flight primarily deals with the following themes: The Power of A Dream, Conflict Resolution, Decision Making, Forgiveness, Overcoming Obstacles, Skill-set Development, and S.T.E.A.M. (Science, Technology, Engineering, Arts and Math). What themes did you notice? Here are a few to get you started.

Theme 1:

The Power of A Dream
Schuyler Watkins has a dream which helps her navigate through the world. Her brother, Tyler has a problem trying to discover his dream. How can a dream help you focus your life? How can a dream help you to overcome challenges, obstacles and adversity?

Theme 2:
Conflict Resolution

Here are a few conflicts from the story: Schuyler's internal conflict, her conflict with Tyler, their conflict with their parents. What other conflicts did you see? How does each character deal with conflict? What place does 'understanding' have in resolving them? How do you deal with conflict? Come up with 3 ways to resolve conflict so that you and the other person can benefit?

Theme 3:
Decision Making

How we choose often determines where we end up in life. Each character has to make a series of choices. How would you rate the quality of their choices? Which would you classify as good and bad? Which are hard to tell what the outcome will be? How do you rate the quality of your own decision making? What changes can you make to help ensure that you 'fly' in life?

Theme 4:

Forgiveness

Forgiveness is one of the most powerful abilities that we have. When we use it, it frees us up. When we withold it, unforgiveness traps us in a prison of our own making. Which characters have to deal with choosing between forgivess and unforgiveness? What is the end result for them? How do you define forgiveness? Do you easily forgive others who have wronged you? Why or why not? And do you see the two words in the word "FOR-GIVE"?

Theme 5:

Skill-set Discovery & Development
Schuyler makes several discoveries about her talents. How does her discovery change the trajectory of her life? What does she do to develop her skills? Who helps her along the way? What is the end result? What are you good at? What can you do to develop your skills? How can you discover talents you may not know you have? What is the benefit of developing your skills and talents?

Theme 6:

S.T.E.A.M.
How does Science, Technology, Engineering, Arts and Math impact this story? Which characters use STEAM to solve their problems? How can you use STEAM principles in your life? Are all students capable of learning STEAM? Why or Why not?

140

ACKNOWLEDGMENTS

This is the first book in the Speedsuit Powers Expanded Universe! It has been a journey to get to this point.

I would like to thank my wife, Ijnanya. You constantly push and inspire me to be the best I can be in life and in my creative pursuits. Thank you for making time to listen to me read scenes and talk through this process. Without you, I could not have made it.

I would like to thank Monique Tabbs for suggesting I create a story with a female protagonist, once my Speedsuit Powers Trilogy was complete! And thank you for reviewing this story. I hope you like Schuyler Watkins!

Thank you Frank Gomez! Your review of this story and your great input has proven to be—as always—invaluable! Onward and upward!

Finally, I want to give a BIG thank you to Ms. Ardel' Paschal P. Sampson for agreeing to be the "face" of Schuyler Watkins on the front and back cover of this book. You truly exemplify a strong, motivated and independent young woman. I look forward to seeing where God takes you in life!

ABOUT THE AUTHOR

Allen Paul Weaver III is an author, speaker and filmmaker. He holds a BA in Speech Communication from Bethune-Cookman University. He also holds a Master of Divinity degree in Theology from Colgate Rochester Crozer Divinity School.

Allen is an avid writer and lover of books - especially comic books. As a teen, he didn't like reading (although he could read well.) One thing he noticed as he devoured comics and science fiction books was the thin representation of key characters who looked like him and shared elements of his life experience.

During the early 2000's, while working as a youth director in the South Bronx, Allen saw the need to create a story which could inspire, motivate and educate entire communities to break through the opposition they faced in order to "Run their Dreams."

Shortly thereafter, the concept for Speedsuit Powers was born. Six years later, in December 2009, Book One of the Trilogy was released. During 2011-2012 Allen adapted Book One into the independent film, *Speedsuit*. He then finished writing Book Two and Three, releasing them in June 2015 and December 2016.

He is excitedly writing additional stories for his Speedsuit Powers Expanded Universe as he seeks to make his works a household name; especially in communities of Color.

Allen enjoys drawing, watching films, indoor skydiving, and traveling with his wife and son. To date, he has traveled to seven African countries, Europe and China.

Find out more about SPT at: www.AllenPaulWeaver3.com.

Flying High:

An interview with Author,
Allen Paul Weaver III

Q: Why write a story about flight?

APW3: Schuyler's love for flight is actually my own... I have been captivated by things that fly since I was 4 years old. For a while now, I have wanted to write this type of story which explores how a dream— no matter how unusual—could help a person navigate life's issues and one day would come true in some form. And I think about those stories which inspired me as a child... they always had a bit of the "fantastic" to them. I hope Flight does the same for those who read it.

Q: If flying is your dream, how did you end up with a female protagonist?

APW3: Initially, when I started drafting the early outline for this story, the protagonist was going to be male. However, after I released Book 3 of my Speedsuit Powers Trilogy, a female friend came to me and suggested that the next main character in my new book be a young woman. When she said that and I thought about it, it made sense since I had just spent 8 years crafting a trilogy where the two main characters were both young men.

Creating a female character and giving her my love for flight, granted a unique opportunity. Even though Schuyler is African American (like me), she is still a young woman, which brings its own set of challenges and opportunities. This was something I felt I could explore. And in this time of black girl and woman empowerment, I am excited to add a creative work which can help inspire girls to pursue their dreams. I am a firm believer that girls are just as capable as boys. In my experience, they are often more capapble, but are not always granted the same opportunities to excel.

Q: Why are dreams so important to you?

APW3: Having a serious dream has a powerful way of elevating your life above the problems you face. Having a dream supplies motivation, passion and drive, where they may not normally exist under the circumstances. Everything else can be going wrong in your life, but the right dream helps refocus your perspective so you can endure pressure, weather the storms and come out better and not bitter.

One of my favorite movies is Akeelah and the Bee. In the story, Akeelah has her problems, but discovers she's gifted at spelling. Initially, that doesn't seem like much, but it opens the door to a wider world of opportunity which helps her rise above the obstacles in her life. And as she pursues that dream, her rising helps her family, her community and even those who oppose her to aspire to more in their own lives. It's a wonderful message about the power of dreams. And we need more of those messages in the world right now. I hope Flight sparks the hearts, minds and imaginations of readers to do similar things with their own lives.

Q: We see in this story that having a dream is crucial, but it is not the only thing that is necessary for success. What are some necessary "success steps?"

APW3: Right. Some people don't have any dreams at all. Others do, but don't know how to pursue them. It is that process of pursuing the dream that is the other side of the coin that is so crucial. Just having a dream doesn't mean we puruse it. Here are some steps I use to pursue my dreams. It's the acronym **R.U.N.**

Research: Whatever your dream is in life, you must first do research. (This is where Google is your friend)! Find out everything you can about what it is you want to do. What are the educational requirements? What training can you do now? Are their Youtube videos you can watch to give you a headstart on preparation? When you research what you say you want to do, you may decide, "Yep, this is what I like!" or "No... this isn't what I thought it was." Doing the research helps you "chart the course" you need to take to make the dream a reality. It gives you a map/blueprint which is extremely valuable for a successful outcome.

Unify: Now that you have a sense of what is required to reach your dream, you must begin to unify your life around the requirements in order to begin the process of making your dream a reality. Here, your daily schedule matters. Basically, your most valuable commodity is your time, so you want to use your time wisely, in service of the dream. Go to your classes. Get extra training. Don't spend the bulk of your time doing activities which don't give you a return on your investment. For example, instead of spending the day binge-watching your favorite tv show, use a large chunk of that time to further develop the skills you need to pursue your dream. Unify your life!

Network: Most of the time, a dream is not achieved in isolation. Once you have done the RESEARCH to help chart the course towards your dream, and you have begun to spend time UNIFYING your life around the dream, then you need to start meeting people who can help further your movement towards the dream. No one can "run" your dream for you, but when people who love and care about you see that you are serious about pursuing your dream, they will bend over backwards to help you get there. So, find out who can help you. Find out who is already doing what you desire to do and see if you can meet to ask questions and learn about their journey. Meet people in order to find places to volunteer your time so you can gain valuable experience. Also, realize when you NETWORK, that it isn't all about what you can get, but it's also about the value you can bring and how you can be a blessing to the people you meet while pursuing your dream.

If you learn how to "R.U.N. your dreams," you will greatly increase the likelihood of being successful in any endeavor.

Q: There's some interesting flight technology introduced in this story. What kind of research did you do?

APW3: I have been studying flight for years (airplanes, helicopters, insects, jetpacks, wingsuits, etc). As I prepared to write this story, I did notice that there is a convergence of technology happening. People are actually creating inventions which are enabling them to fly in more practical ways (than the rocketbelt which only has enough fuel for 26 seconds of flight time). I mention several of them in the story. Technology is finally catching up with our imagination. New motors, rotors and ways of thinking about flight are opening up new possibilities. I think, within the next 10 years or so, if technology continues to advance as it has been, more and more people will have access to new flight technology.

At the very least, I want to be a part of that larger narrative as humanity seeks after personal human flight. So, I decided to write my flight ideas into story form. My hope is one day, in the near future, to actually create these designs for real.

Q: What is your writing process like?

APW3: Well, for one, I don't often write in chronological order. In the past I've compared my process to "connect the dots." I would write wherever there was inspiration and then work to fill in the gaps. Now, my process has a few more elements to it.

First, I write an outline of the story: the anticipated number of chapters I think the book will have, and the major plot elements which happen in each chapter (2-4 sentences each). Doing the outline helps give me a sense of pacing and an overall direction for the story. Then I write out the scenes—wherever the inspiration comes—until I have a completed rough draft. Then I read it for gaps that need to be filled until all of the "dots" are connected. After making those tweaks and producing a 1st and 2nd draft, I will have 1-2 people read the story and provide feedback. Then, based on their feedback, I make further adjustments for a 3rd and 4th draft. Then it goes to my editor who looks for spelling, punctuation, grammar and story issues. Once the editor returns it, I make those changes and finalize everything for printing. All in all, the story typically goes through a minimum of 7 drafts before it's ready for publication.

Q: FLIGHT is an extention of your Speedsuit Powers Trilogy. Why did you write SPT?

APW3: Actually, I never set out to write a trilogy. Initially, it was just going to be one book, but I left it with an open ending just in case I would do another one. The response from readers was so tremendous, I knew a second book had to be written. Then, as I wrote, it became clear it was becoming a trilogy. So, the entire process happened very organically.

Having said that, at the time when the idea was birthed in me, I was living in the South Bronx, working with youth. Having grown up in the suburbs, I had been able to travel and see a wider part of the world. But in the Bronx, I was encountering kids who only knew their neighborhood. Many had never been to a museum or flown in an airplane or done much outside of their urban experience. I would meet families who were struggling with things I had never experienced. And I would go to schools to speak to guidance counselors on behalf of students, only to get the runaround, because guidance counselors were swamped in a school system that was overcrowded, underfunded and under resourced.

Now, sure, there were kids I met and worked with who "shined" and did well in school and were able to rise above the negative aspects of their urban context, but these seemed more the exceptions rather than the rule. With more and more interactions with youth, young adults and parents, I was moved to do something more... but I didn't know what

147

"more" was.

Then the idea came for writing a novel that would hopefully inspire, motivate and educate young readers towards greatness. It was exciting to think that the book could help to multiply my efforts to reach people. So, I developed an outline for the story (guy from the suburbs moves to the inner city and encounters a school bully...) And after a lot of work, Speedsuit Powers: Book I was born. As I said, the response was tremendous. People were contacting me saying their sons and daughters were loving the story and reading it in a matter of hours and days! It was written for urban middle school boys, but people from different age groups and ethnicities were loving the story as well. Readers were asking, "what happens next?" So, I kept writing and decided, to follow Curtis and Treyshawn from adolescents to young adulthood. And along the way, the story addresses a multiplicity of themes from school bullying to conflict resolution, decision making and identity formation, trauma recovery, S.T.E.A.M. (Science, technology, engineering, arts, mathamatics), and a host of other issues.

Q: You have always inlcuded elements of your Christian Faith in your Speedsuit Powers Trilogy. And you do so in this story. Why is that important to you?

APW3: For all of the things I'm interested in—and there are many—from comics to science, to filmmaking, traveling, drawing, music, languages, etc... the most important "interest" to me is my faith. Jesus Christ is the single most important person in my life. If it wasn't for his intervention when I attempted suicide back in 1992, I wouldn't be here to have any interests. So, my mind is always on Jesus no matter what I do.

So for me, as a writer, to not include elements of the most important aspect of my existence, is like trying to describe breathing to someone, but leaving out the fact that Oxygen is required for us to breathe.

Q: How did you decide to create the expanded Speedsuit Powers world?

APW3: When I started writing Speedsuit Powers: Book One, I also had other characters and stories that were unrelated to the trilogy. I figured, after I finished with SP, I would focus on these other ideas. But, as I wrote Books 2 and 3 of the trilogy, it became apparent that with a bit of tweaking, I could incorporate these other stories into the world of Speedsuit Powers (much like what happens in the worlds of Marvel or DC comics - multiple characters and storylines that happen in the same world with minimal or significant crossover). So, as the trilogy was developing, I began to incorporate a few characters into the story knowing after the trilogy was complete, I would like to do spinoff books to explore new adventures. Right now, I have about 7 additional stories to tell.

Q: What has this writing journey been like for you?

APW3: [Laughing} This has been a long, tedious, arduous, gut-wrenching, wonderful, amazing, satisfying journey!

I never saw myself as an author. And when I wrote my very first book, Transition: Breaking Through the Barriers, I never thought I would write another book. And then SP: Book One came and I never thought I'd write another. Now, the story ideas keep coming and I'm just trying to keep up!

Writing a story is very personal to me because a lot of my heart and soul goes into it. I remember after writing the outline for SP: Book One, I was going to hire a ghostwriter because I felt I couldn't write well enough to do the story justice. But my wife told me, "you should write it because it's a story that's very dear to your heart." She was right. So, writing is personal. Because of that, it can be a bit scary to put a book out into the world... you hope people will like it and it doesn't get rejected.

Some people have rejected the stories I've written, but I try not to take that personal. Early on, not taking it personal was very hard to do. But, I realize that "people are people." Everyone has their own individual tastes for what they like and don't like. I try to gain feedback for why someone doesn't like what I write. If it's valid, I keep it. If not, I throw it away.

So, this journey has been wonderful (in the grand scheme of things) and uncomfortable because to create and share means coming outside of my comfort zone. But it is well worth it! I look forward to seeing where things end up.

Q: What is one way this journey has pushed you outside your comfort zone?

APW3: Well, I love books that include artwork which helps readers visualize the story. I've always loved to draw and have been drawing since I was a child. But, my self-esteem has consistently been low about my drawing skills because I often would compare them to professional artists. So, when I wrote SP: Book One, I did a number of concept sketches of various scenes (I'm a very visual person). But I hired a professional freelance artist (Shawn Alleyne) to fully develop those concepts (which is shown on each chapter title page in Book One).

After we went through that process, Shawn said to me, "Allen, you draw very well. You should consider putting some of your artwork in your book." His words were a huge encouragement for me. Still, I was afraid to do so. However, when I was working on SP: Book 2, Shawn was not available to do the artwork. So, with much prayer [laughing], I decided to do the artwork myself. Then I also, hired a 3D artist (Jeff Tyler) to bring some of the concept drawings of the suit and several buildings to life in 3D. By SP: Book 3, I was much more confident with drawing the characters.

I will never forget sitting on the train, working on a drawing for the book and a woman sitting across from me asked, "Are you an artist for Marvel or DC comics?" Talk about putting a smile on my face! I still have a ways to go before I'm drawing at that level! (smile) So, this writing journey has also helped me even more so as an artist. I will keep working to push the boundaries of my drawing skills and to work with others who can help to visually bring the world of Speedsuit Powers to life.

Q: What advice would you give to aspiring writers?

APW3: Write. Write. And write some more. When you write a story, don't initially be so focused on "what am I going to say?" and "how do I organize it?" Many people who want to write tell me, "I don't know where to start!" I like to say, "start writing where the inspiration is."

Just get your thoughts down on paper. Then you can massage them by editing and organizing them into a particular order. Also, after you write something, find someone you trust and ask them to read what you have written. Ask them for an honest critique. No one gets better as a writer if they can't take an honest critique and make the adjustment. Most of the time, when I write something I think is brilliant and send it to my editor, it comes back with a lot of red ink and suggestions for making it better. That used to bother me at first, but I learned over time that is what makes a better writer.

So, write, write, write... and then write some more. Write what you know. AND... write where you want to go. (In other words, write what you don't know but may be interested in.) You can write about your life or about some far-off world... just be true to the story you want to tell.

Also, when you are ready to put your writing out to the world, do your best to make sure you have no grammar/punctuation errors. You want to make the best presentation possible in order to reach the largest audience possible. Putting your work out with obvious errors tells the reader that you don't care about the quality of your story. Words mean something. Punctuation means something. They both help to communicate ideas from your mind to the mind of the reader. So, do your best in all areas of your writing experience.

Finally... have fun. Enjoy the process. When the words come easy and when they don't. The process is growing you.

Finally... finally... never throw an idea away. You may come up with an idea that is unusable for the particular story you are working on. If so, just file it away somewhere safe. You never know where that idea may lead at a later time.

Finally... finally... finally... there is no time like the present to begin writing. So, don't make excuses. I believe everyone has at least one book in them. So, get to it! I look forward to seeing what you create!

www.ingramcontent.com/pod-product-compliance
Lightning Source LLC
Chambersburg PA
CBHW071916220626
47052CB00002B/375